*delicate monsters*

Also by Stephanie Kuehn

*Charm & Strange*

*Complicit*

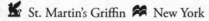

# *delicate monsters*

Stephanie Kuehn

St. Martin's Griffin New York

This is a work of fiction. All of the characters, organizations, and events portrayed in this novel are either products of the author's imagination or are used fictitiously.


Printed in the United States of America. For information, address St. Martin's Press, 175 Fifth Avenue, New York, N.Y. 10010.

www.stmartins.com

Designed by Molly Rose Murphy

The Library of Congress Cataloging-in-Publication Data is available upon request.

ISBN 978-1-250-06384-7 (hardcover)
ISBN 978-1-4668-6885-4 (e-book)

St. Martin's Griffin books may be purchased for educational, business, or promotional use. For information on bulk purchases, please contact the Macmillan Corporate and Premium Sales Department at 1-800-221-7945, extension 5442, or write to specialmarkets@macmillan.com.

First Edition: June 2015

10 9 8 7 6 5 4 3 2 1

For my father, who taught me to say what I mean

# *part 1*

## Ennui

Tu le connais, lecteur, ce monstre délicat,—Hypocrite lecteur,—mon semblable,—mon frère!

—Charles Baudelaire,
*Les Fleurs du mal*

# *chapter one*

A ropes course was a shitty place for self-discovery. Seventeen-year-old Sadie Su understood she was meant to think otherwise, but (1) she had no interest in introspection and (2) even if she did, what the hell was the point? This loamy godforsaken spot in the Santa Cruz Mountains was a playground for perceived risk only. Nothing here was real. Nothing was transformative.

True change required true danger.

Sadie shifted her legs and tugged to loosen the straps on the safety harness she wore. Blood was being constricted from places she thought blood needed to go.

When she felt more comfortable and no one was looking, Sadie turned away from the group. She sidled a little ways down the hillside, black sheep leaving the flock, before edging out of sight of the ropes course, the towering redwood trees, and the other girls from the wilderness camp. They were teenagers like her, the girls, all supposedly "troubled." Only unlike Sadie, they were wide-eyed and tragic, fragile, herdlike things, brimming with stories of Painful Childhoods about who'd touched them where or hit them or abandoned them and a million other sad sap excuses for why they did the Things They Did. Sadie couldn't be bothered to take it all in. Misery repulsed her. Self-pity even more. She especially couldn't understand the counselors and therapists who *chose* to work here. It made Sadie shudder to think about. If there was a special circle of hell for girls like her, and she suspected there might be, there was no doubt her eternity would be spent having to listen to other people's problems.

Sadie kept walking along the dirt path. Her steps were light and calculated. Wind blew up the mountain and through the trees. It smelled like the ocean, although she couldn't see the ocean, and Sadie reached to dig the nylon harness even further out of her crotch. Then she fished a soft pack of American Spirits and a book of matches from the front pocket of her coveralls. Crumbs of tobacco fell onto the ground. Brown curls littering the gray earth.

"You'll start a fire," a voice said.

Sadie looked up. One of the other girls from the camp—Laura? Lara? Laurel? whatever—was standing on the path. She was probably on her way back from the bathroom.

"Is that a warning or a declarative?" Sadie asked.

"It's common sense," the girl said, folding her arms in a way meant as threatening.

Sadie sighed. She found threats a curious thing because she didn't respond to them the way she was meant to. They didn't make her heart race or her pits sweat. And they didn't make her mouth fumble to come up with flush-faced apologies. No, threats made Sadie's skin grow cold and her brain grow mean. As if to prove her point, she reached up to light her cigarette, then threw the glowing match into the dry brush.

"Nothing common about it," she said.

Fourteen minutes and two American Spirits later, Sadie made her way back to the ropes course. The counselors sniffed the air like they knew what she'd been doing, but said nothing. They couldn't change her, and they weren't paid enough to try. Besides, they already had their hands full trying to coax the rest of the girl-herd up into the trees where they were meant to leap into free fall, crab walk across high-strung cables, and conquer their innermost fears. A losing battle. Some of the girls cried and trembled, refusing to move. Still others squared their jaws and pushed their shoulders back, going for brazen courage, but failing hard. They had it all wrong, of course. Bravery wasn't required to conquer fear.

Indifference was.

One of the course leaders, a middle-aged man, and a guileless one at that, strode right over to Sadie. He wore his knee socks rolled up and a full-brimmed hat. A patch of zinc oxide striped his nose.

"You ready to give it a try, sweetheart?" His smile was warm and wide enough to show his teeth.

Sadie gave her own smile right back. "Sure, I'm ready."

"What's your name?"

"Sadie," she said. "Sadie Su."

"You Chinese?"

"Half."

"You don't look Chinese."

Sadie's smile grew bigger. "That's what my daddy says."

The man blinked, but didn't respond. Instead, he reached out to clip his belay rope to her loosened harness. He did it as if it were something he'd done a million times. As if an act of connection were as common as cruelty.

As if.

Sadie stood very still. At the clanking of their carabiners, she felt no rubbing of their fates, no flutter of destiny. The man droned on with his droll safety instructions, words full of caution, like the way he wore his clothes, and when he was done, she turned and scrambled up the footholds of an old-growth sequoia.

At the top of the ladder, Sadie paused and looked down. She had to be eighty feet in the air. She felt the burning eyes of the other girls, watching her from the forest floor below, like heat rising from dying coals. Maybe they wished she'd fall. She didn't doubt it. She'd wish it, too, if she were them.

The wind blew harder, fiercer. Off in the distance a hint of blue-gray was visible between the trees. Sadie squinted, and there it was at last—the Pacific Ocean, wild and abstract, like something from a dream. With a groan, she used her arms to haul herself up onto the flat wood platform above her. Then she walked to the edge and bent her legs.

When she felt like it, she jumped.

The evening after the ropes course was Sadie's last night at the wilderness camp. She'd done her time here, ten long weeks, and now she lay in her cabin in the dark with her eyes open, restless and unable to sleep. What was next for her? What did she need? Answers, conviction, eluded her, forging a loose sense of confusion she was unaccustomed to. She'd always faced uncertainty head on, only this time, she wasn't going anywhere uncertain.

Sadie was going home.

It was a hard truth that in the morning, she would return to her family's vast wine country estate, four years older than when she'd left and pretty much none the wiser. In that time she'd attended and been asked to leave three separate boarding schools, including one in Düsseldorf and one in Paris. The last had been in New York State, a crisp-aired campus ringed by apple orchards and brick homes with woodstoves, all tucked in a sun-dappled turn of the Hudson Valley. The things she'd done there not only ensured that no other private school would take her, they'd gotten her sent *here* as part of the legal settlement. Only *here* was as useless as *there*. Everything, everywhere, was geared toward giving her things: tools, skills, knowledge, new ways of being. All garbage. Sadie figured you couldn't take in what you weren't missing in the first place. She liked the way she was. It was other people she had a problem with.

A mile to the south, in a row of tent cabins scattered among lush ferns on the edge of a slick rock creek bed, sat the wilderness camp's male counterpart. Every night, the boys came knocking for the girls. Like Pavlov's dogs, they showed up, a steady stream of slobbering, dick-wielding fuckups and addicts and head cases. The girls in Sadie's cabin always went with them. Always did things in preparation that made her stomach sick—like plucking their eyebrows and shaving the hair between their legs and ass cheeks.

But on that last night, one of the boys came for Sadie. His name was Chad. He had a peach-fuzz mustache and a row of pimples on his neck. She went with him into the woods, onto the bare ground beneath the stars.

"I won't fuck you," she told him.

"Then I want a blow job," he said.

Sadie wouldn't do that either and whining didn't help his cause. But when she unzipped his jeans and reached her hand in to touch him, Chad shut up fast. She sat up while she did it, the touching, keeping her eyes open so she could watch him go from very bold to very still. Sadie liked watching. There was power in bearing witness.

Pleasure, too. After, she hiked her own skirt up, crawled on top, and pressed herself against him. That was all it took.

That was all she needed.

"Why are you here?" Chad whispered, as they lay together in the dirt, side by side, like animals. Sadie had her cigarettes out again and gave one to Chad when he asked.

"I'm leaving tomorrow. Going home."

"That doesn't answer my question."

"I got kicked out of boarding school. Third one in four years. Only thing left is the public alternative."

"That's it?"

"I tried to kill somebody," Sadie said softly, and Chad laughed in a way that made her want to strangle him. He laughed like he didn't believe her.

"Yeah, me too." Cigarette gripped between teeth and lips, he held his bare wrists up in the moonlight so that she could see the scars there, jagged pink lines that resembled streaks of lightning flashing across the morning sky.

"That's not what I meant," Sadie said, although this was partially a lie. She did mean it that way, but she meant it another way, too, and she wanted Chad to understand that. She wanted him to know that she was both worse and different than him, different than everyone here, with their sadness and their anger and all their messy *needs*. It was bad enough, her rubbing against him like she had, taking what she wanted, just because she'd felt hot and aching and driven.

Hurting other people wasn't all that different, though. That was also a form of taking and she did it all the time. Sometimes she wished she didn't. Sometimes the things she took were unforgivable and she'd give anything to have better control over herself.

Then again, sometimes Sadie was bored.

And oftentimes, that was more than enough.

# chapter two

*What did it feel like to fall in love?*

This was a thought so novel and jarring that eighteen-year-old Emerson Tate nearly fell straight from his lawn chair into the soft grass of Ryan Bloom's stately Sonoma backyard. It was a slow slip, no drunken pratfall, just a teetering of Emerson's oversized frame and limbs, then an overcorrection to keep his drink from sloshing over, but in the end he caught himself. Stayed upright and off the ground. Relieved, he sank deeper into the low-slung canvas seat and let the warm haze of booze and late-summer sun weight him down.

Let his wistful longing pulse through him like an anchor scraping the pebbly bottom of the deepest lake.

A roar of laughter came from the direction of the pool. Emerson's head snapped up, along with his hackles and insecurities. Were they laughing at him? He couldn't swim, a fact that embarrassed him badly, a stark reminder of the suburban normality his family had never known. But no, it was just a group of guys horsing around in the deep end of the Blooms' Olympic-sized pool with a sopping wet football. Bryan James pulled his trunks down and dove beneath the water. His bare ass bobbed around on the surface like a lost white whale. More laughter. A few shrieks and catcalls from the girls. Emerson felt himself relax again. The air hung ripe with the scent of coconut oil and pot.

*That should be a candle flavor,* he thought. *Mass produced and marketed. The nostalgia line: Eighteen and life . . .*

This was summer's end for him, for them, as true as any other. Sonoma High had just finished its first official day of fall classes. The pool party was a way for the senior class to forget about the burdens of the impending year, what with its college applications and achievement exams, its disappointments and acceptance. The inevitable goodbyes. It was too much to face head-on, without the lights dimmed a little.

Gulping down more of his drink—heavy vodka, light orange juice—Emerson shifted his gaze from the pool back to the long patch of manicured bluegrass where a badminton net stretched between two elm trees. The net had a tear on one side, a sag in the middle, but none of this stopped the two girls with racquets who were swatting a birdie back and forth and giggling over the word *shuttlecock*. The girl closest to Emerson held a gin and tonic in one hand, and she wore her feet bare. Her name was May, and she was his opposite in every possible sense. Where Emerson was pale, blond, big, and clumsy, May was dark skin, soft breasts, lean and full of grace. She was a delicate turn of the ankle. She was ice slowly melting. Her hair, a mess of wild black curls, bounced and glistened. Like the soft trampolining of his soul.

Watching her move, Emerson felt his body stir, awaken.

Every part of him.

This, he told himself, this was the beginning of love. It had to be. The way he felt, like his heart was setting down roots in a bare dirt hole he didn't know needed to be filled, it was transcendent.

*It feels honest.*

*It feels like truth.*

"How many drinks does that make, Tate? You going for a record?"

"Huh?" In a shuddering instant, Emerson went from lust to shame. He set his screwdriver down in haste. Prayed it didn't tip over and spill.

"Nah, I'm not hassling you, man. Come on. It's senior year. There's no such thing as moderation." Trey Bornstein, who was dressed in pink madras shorts and nothing else, slapped him on the back, then reached down with a bottle of Stoli and poured. He filled Emerson's glass to the brim and then some. "Whoops. Just watering the lawn. Maybe it's good for it. Think plants can get drunk?"

Emerson shook his head. He had a suspicion the vodka had come from the bar inside the house, which meant Ryan Bloom would be pissed when he found out. His mom was more territorial than most. Wealth did that, Emerson knew, made rich people care more about losing what they had than other people. Just stepping into the Bloom home meant not wearing shoes and sitting on plastic slipcovers. It meant guest orange juice and Otter Pops instead of fresh squeezed and hand-churned ice cream. Mrs. Bloom even kept a set of cheap swim trunks in the pool house so that no one would accidentally walk off with a pair of Ryan's brand-name board shorts. Emerson highly doubted the Stoli was her guest vodka.

Trey pulled up his own chair and sat across from him. The wind shifted and brought with it the sharp stench of grapes fermenting on the vine from down off the hillside. Emerson felt a wave of sudden sickness. He picked his drink up and sniffed at it, wanting to inhale wafts of chilled citrus. Not wanting to vomit in the grass.

"New girl's a bitch, man," Trey said. He leaned back and put his legs up on a padded ottoman. He had the same basketball height as Emerson—they played together—but Trey's legs were thin, wiry, like a thoroughbred, coated in red-brown hairs that matched the ones on his head.

"Mmm," Emerson said, not sure if he dared open his mouth or not. What he wanted to do was keep looking at May, the girl he'd known since sophomore year, but had never truly *seen*. Until now. Maybe it was something in the way she moved. Pure feminine harmony. Why hadn't he noticed it before?

"She says she knows you."

Emerson risked a sip of vodka. "Who?"

Trey had a way with restlessness; he'd mastered it. Before he answered, he pushed his hair back and scratched his balls. He picked a scab until it bled. Finally he pointed. "Her. Over there."

Emerson turned his head reluctantly. Sure enough, a girl stood in the corner by the fence, smoking. Short, thin, she had dark hair and mirrored sunglasses. Her bikini top was black and her tits were small. Smaller than he liked.

"I don't know any new girl," he said.

"She says she knows you. Name's Sadie something . . . Sadie—"

"Sadie Su?" Emerson peered closer. *Shit.* It'd been years, but it could be her.

"So you do know her?" Trey's voice held a note of betrayal. "Like I said, she's a bitch. Must be dumb as sin, too. I mean, who changes schools when they're a senior?"

Who indeed? Emerson didn't know and didn't care, but the thing was, Sadie wasn't new. She was *old*. She lived here, had always lived here, only not right in town, but out in the valley with her rich parents. They owned this ridiculous vineyard, despite not being vintners. It was the kind of home you saw photographed in magazines, immaculate sprawling grounds dotted with statuaries and teeming with hired help. Years ago, when he was just a kid, Emerson had spent a lot of time out there on the Su property. Every day after school, for a good six months, he and Sadie had been thrust together for hours. Every day they'd talk and play and—

A scrabble of dread ran up Emerson's spine.

Or maybe it was guilt.

"I don't want to talk about Sadie," he said.

Trey shrugged, looked away. "Yeah, fine. Whatever."

Emerson settled back in the chair and tried to reclaim his sense of peace. Once again, he fixed his gaze on the badminton game. On gin cocktails and a summer breeze. On the sleek, sun-roasted girl he was falling in love with and who just might love him back.

If only she knew how he felt.

If only he would tell her.

Miles was already home by the time Emerson stumbled in, way late, with his head pounding and legs sore from having walked all the way across town to where their dilapidated apartment complex sat in the shadow of a glowing Walgreens and a run-down Pizza Hut. Emerson was equal parts drunk and hung over, which was a bitch of a way to start the new school year, but at least he'd known better than to drive. His fifteen-year-old brother, who wore his blond hair too long and never cleaned beneath his nails, sat perched on a barstool like a spooked owl. He'd made food of some sort. Burned it, too, from the smell. What appeared to be angel-hair pasta and soy sauce.

Emerson took a deep breath. Promised himself he wouldn't get angry. "Why're you eating that crap?"

Miles shrugged. "Hungry."

"You're gonna get sick."

Miles shrugged again, skinny shoulders rising up with the sort of ennui he was known for. Fifteen going on fifty, Emerson knew three things to be true about his younger brother: First, he was sickly, something Emerson had come to believe was just a part of his nature the way impulsivity and overthinking were a part of his. Over the years, Miles's list of diagnosed ailments had grown faster than he had—night terrors, abdominal migraines, separation anxiety, failure to thrive, wheezes, rashes, fevers, impetigo, now possibly this celiac thing. When they were younger, their mom had been blamed for his frailties, but Emerson knew she'd done nothing but try and make him better. He'd testified to that in court.

The second thing about Miles was that he didn't like other people and didn't care to. Perhaps this was the result of their father's death, eight years prior. It was something that had made Emerson himself go a little crazy. No kid expected his seemingly healthy father to expire without warning one rainy Wednesday night while working on his Mustang in the family garage. And no kid expected to be shielded from the cause of his seemingly healthy father's death for reasons that had never been fully explained. It wasn't until years later that Emerson stumbled onto the disturbing truth: His dad hadn't succumbed to a heart attack or stroke or any kind of accident. No, his death had been a deliberate act, the calculated outcome of starting the engine, attaching a rubber hose to the tailpipe and running it back into the driver's-side window.

Lastly, for all his oddities, Emerson felt his younger brother was destined for . . . something. Greatness? Notoriety? Emerson hadn't pinpointed it yet, but there was a force within Miles that both awed and frightened him. Emerson wasn't awed or frightened easily, so these were definitely feelings he took note of.

"How was school?" Emerson asked, walking into the kitchen to pour a glass of water from the tap. He figured he needed to drink at least a gallon or two to even think about functioning in the morning. "Didn't see you all day."

"I was there," Miles said, and although Emerson waited, no further elaboration came. That was the extent of their communication. A few minutes later, Miles went pale. He gripped his stomach, slid from the barstool, and bolted for the bathroom. He didn't come out again. He probably wouldn't for a long time. Emerson cleaned the kitchen and put the dishes away so their mom wouldn't have to when she got back from her shift at the nursing home. He owed her that. He owed her more. He and Miles didn't have much after their father's death, but what they did was the result of her work ethic, her ability to move forward and not look back.

Finishing with the last of the dishes, Emerson went to the small room he shared with Miles and closed the door. He lay on a sagging twin bed. He turned the ceiling fan on high.

His head spun from the Stoli and the heat.

Despair took many forms in this room. In shadows and memories best left forgotten. In shame, dark and cloying. Tonight despair came for Emerson cloaked in the knowledge that he'd have to get up and do the whole school thing all over again tomorrow. And the next day. And the day after that. The only bright spot in Emerson's life, besides basketball, was May—the girl, not the month.

Thinking of her, the way her body curved and the way he liked it, Emerson slid his pants off, then his boxers down. He longed for a real connection with May, of course. He wanted Friday night dates and lazy afternoon sex and whispered phone calls after curfew. He wanted those things with a need as bright and frantic as life itself, but tonight Emerson chased simpler dreams, using his hand and his loneliness to lope dutifully after brief fantasy and even briefer pleasure.

He longed mostly for the sleep that would come after.

# *chapter three*

It was the third day of school when Sadie got called in to the vice principal's office to discuss her educational "strategy." As if educating her might be akin to warfare, requiring hawkish tactics and well-planned maneuvers. Although considering what she'd done to get kicked out of her last school, that approach might not be unwarranted. Sadie wondered what Sun Tzu might have to say on the matter.

*Practice dissimulation, and you will succeed.*

There was no doubt this meeting was going to be a bitch and a half, but Sadie was glad to be attending alone and without her mother, who liked to make a big showy production out of everything and get lawyers involved. Sadie wasn't into that. Throwing money around didn't always mean you got your way, and it didn't make people respect you. Collateral was more important.

Leverage, the most.

Sadie strolled through the halls of Sonoma High at roughly the pace of the continental drift. She coolly eyed the students around her. Did they know who she was or what she'd done? The story of how Roman Bender had nearly died in an unfortunate "prank" last winter had made headlines in New York, but did it make waves out here? She doubted it. The California wine country didn't keep up with things like prep school hijinks or erudite tradition or how long-term exposure to the snow and subzero temps could lead to heart arrhythmia and frostbit fingers. It didn't keep up with much at all.

This whole place was gross, she decided, stagnant in its banality. Not that the fancy boarding schools had been great or anything, but at least there'd been a sense of *relevance.* There was nothing relevant in Sonoma. Beneath the glitzy wine industry and quaint tourism pooled a dark futility, a cruel sort of helplessness. It lurked in corners. It oozed from hormones.

When she got to the office, the school secretary waved Sadie right in. She was late, which was good, because if there was one thing Sadie hated, it was being made to wait for others.

The vice principal was an older woman. Well put together at first glance, but there were other hints Sadie quickly picked up on: the frayed hem of her houndstooth jacket, a plastic travel mug with a cracked lid that left ring stains on the fake wood-grain desk, a brown-bag lunch she hadn't bothered to refrigerate. Sadie felt both disgust and disappointment. Not for herself, but for the world as a whole. If this woman, with her budget lifestyle and bureaucracy headaches, was meant to be inspirational or, worse, aspirational, it might be better for everyone involved if Russia or North Korea or someone just dropped a bomb on the whole damn place. Put them all out of their misery. American exceptionalism was a mass delusion, Sadie thought. A real sickness. Unless you defined exceptionalism as the ability to bargain shop at Ross and eat Lunchables.

The vice principal prattled on for a bit, first making changes to Sadie's class schedule, then dropping buzzwords like "accountability" and "opportunity" and "appropriate disciplinary action." Sadie made sure to nod along a few times, but she wasn't listening, not really. Not until she heard the words "mandated counseling."

"What was that?" she asked.

"One of your conditions for going here and not Birchwood is that you attend weekly counseling sessions."

Birchwood was the nearby continuation school. AKA fuckup city.

Sadie narrowed her eyes. "Counseling with who?"

The vice principal sat back in her chair. "The school has a psychologist on site. Or you can see a private therapist. Whichever you prefer."

She thought about it. A private therapist meant letting her mom pick one for her. Sadie envisioned sitting across from some large-breasted woman who made her fortune listening to rich matrons bemoan the state of their vaginas. Worse, she'd probably have a water feature in her office and want to talk about chakras.

"I'll see the school one," she said quickly. "Whoever it is."

"Fine." She was handed a vellum card with the name THOMAS MACDOUGALL, PH.D. printed on it. "You can make your own appointment."

"Okay."

When Sadie didn't move, the vice principal leaned forward and made a *scoot scoot* gesture with her hands as the bell rang. "Have a good day, Miss Su."

Dumped back out into the bustling hallway with a printout of her new schedule, Sadie decided she'd make an effort to go to class. That was a big deal for her, effort. If she was genuinely good at something, then she shouldn't have to try. But there was a drumbeat of warning running through her head. It was a soft sound, rolling like the distant wind. The drumbeat told her to *Stay the course. Be good. Be patient.*

It whispered, *You're going to shine.*

It whispered, *Just you wait and see.*

Sadie ducked her head and ran right into Emerson Tate. Her childhood friend.

Or something.

Always the golden boy, now a good foot taller than her and handsome in a dumb kind of way, Emerson looked as surprised as she felt. She didn't show it, though. Unlike him.

"Sadie," he said in a deep voice, rubbing his hand along his stubbled chin before repeating the motion. "I've been looking for you."

"You have? Why?"

"I wanted to say hi. It's been . . . a while. I didn't recognize you at first."

Sadie frowned. She hadn't expected him to recognize her. In fact, she'd sort of counted on it.

"You look different," she told him.

Emerson shifted his weight around. "Yeah, sure. I'm a lot taller. Bigger. Six four. Two hundred twenty pounds."

"That's not what I mean."

They stared at each other.

"I play basketball," he said lamely. "Varsity."

"Oh." Sadie let her eyes sparkle. "So I guess you like niggers now?"

"Wh-what?" Emerson fumbled for his words and Sadie watched his cheeks go red.

She shrugged. "You like basketball, I figure it's a given. I mean, I don't care. I don't have a problem with it. It's just, I remember the way you used to talk about them."

He went even redder. "Well, what are you doing back here? I haven't seen you in forever."

"My folks sent me away to boarding school. Only I did some bad things and it turned out boarding school wanted me even less than my parents. So here I am."

"Our senior year," Emerson said.

"Our senior year," she echoed.

He rubbed his chin again. Looked more uncomfortable than ever. "Well, I guess I'll be seeing you 'round then, Sadie."

"Why I guess you will," she said smoothly.

# chapter four

*Et tu, Brute?*

There were many things about starting his sophomore year at Sonoma High that dissatisfied Miles Tate. The noise. The crowds. The interminable teasing. Last year a group of guys he didn't even know had decided the soft features of his face and overgrown blond hair reminded them of a certain online porn star best known for her athletic blow jobs. Rather than admiration, this resemblance earned him nothing but torment. *Deep Throat,* they'd whisper at him in the hall, in the classroom, in the lunchroom, at the urinals. *Show us how you take it. Suck me. Show me. Do it. You know you want to.*

Well, no. Miles didn't think he wanted to. The act seemed like a messy one and more trouble than it was worth. But those hissing words had shown up again, on the very first morning of classes, along with a crudely drawn image of a jizzing dick, which was scrawled across his locker door. In truth, the drawing more closely resembled an earthworm eating a stick than anything anatomical, but the intent was clear. Miles chose to deal with it the way he dealt with everything: through brooding silence and heavy resignation.

The newest and worst burden of the year, however, was gym class. His advisor had pulled him aside and informed him that he needed PE units in order to graduate. Miles had had no idea. He didn't appreciate what he did with his own body being a requirement for anything, but apparently the matter wasn't up for discussion. In a flustered haste he'd agreed to take fencing, which was a sport he knew nothing about, other than the fact that he'd get to wear a mask.

So now here he was, standing in the Old Gym, sword in hand. Well, a foil, really, and there was a knob on the tip to keep him from killing somebody. The instructor had left the room in search of a missing attendance sheet, and the other fourteen students milled about, looking equally lost and incompetent. They all moved awkwardly in their cushioned uniforms, mesh helmets in hands or on their heads. Sunbeams and dust motes swirled around their bodies like auras.

*"En garde!"* A girl he didn't know lunged forward suddenly and poked Miles in the side with her foil. Hard. It didn't hurt, but he felt a little like barfing, which was how he usually felt when people talked to him or worse, touched him. Still, Miles realized she was being friendly and he, melodramatic. He lifted his own foil up and let her jab at him some more.

Soon those around them had paired off as well. The small gym rattled with the cacophony of shoe-squeak on glossed wood and ring-song of metal on metal. The more Miles parried, the harder the girl thrust, but seeing as he wasn't one for competition or conventional gender roles, he was content to stay on defense.

She jabbed him again and again. In the shoulder. The chest. Twice in the ass. Miles danced on the balls of his feet, mostly for show, but also for reasons not totally clear even to himself. The more he moved, the more it felt like his nerves had become sentient, sprouting jittery little minds of their own. He grew sweaty, then short of breath. These were symptoms he attributed to physical exertion, but when his head began to buzz and his skin went hot and tingly, he understood through a flutter-flap of panic that something else was happening.

Something purposeful.

And real.

Miles stumbled back from the girl and clutched his chest. He felt his heart pounding. He felt people staring. He needed air. Ripping his helmet off and letting it fall to the floor, he strode for the nearest fire exit. The panic bar gave under his weight and the door flew open. No alarm sounded.

The emergency was all in his head.

Stepping out onto the blacktop and into the sunlight, Miles inhaled deeply. He worked to force oxygen to his extremities, his brain, but the heat inside him flared. He was burning up, serious internal combustion. With a gasp, he tipped his head back. Stared at the too-bright sky.

He knew what was coming.

He *knew.*

This vision came down with shooting star speed. It rolled over him, faster than a wish, leaving him sick and sweaty and trembling. The details of what he was seeing were hazy, hazier than usual, indistinct surges of chaos and death. Miles floated choppily in his own consciousness, somewhat aware that the other students from his fencing class had streamed outside to gawk at him, foils still in hand, their eyes wide, their laughter sharp.

Part of him was embarrassed and part of him didn't care because by now a low pulse of electricity was spiraling up his spine and radiating through his limbs, and all Miles wanted was to *see*. But as more and more of his classmates appeared, a swirling parade of white cotton and steel, Miles felt the innermost core of his gut rumble with the pinpoint conviction that whatever was going to happen, whatever pain or tragedy the future held and wanted him to know about beforehand, was directly related to him and the people around him. To the blades in their hands and the curiosity in their minds.

Somewhere, somehow, in the near future, Miles knew, some of them would be winners, some losers, and others, like himself, would be asked to fall on their swords.

# *chapter five*

Saturday afternoon was sunny, clear, and a parade of hot air balloons dotted the blue sky like ornaments on a tree, but there was still something undeniably morbid about driving around in the same '64 dynasty green Mustang convertible his father had offed himself in. It was a feeling Emerson got every time he slid behind the wheel. And it wasn't even the dying part that made it so damn awful. It was the fact that this was the precise spot where his father had decided being dead for himself was better than being alive for his wife and sons.

Maybe there were times suicide made sense. When the immoral choice was moral. Emerson could believe that. But his father was no

Walter White. He hadn't been terminally ill or struggling with addiction or living a dual life where he'd accrued huge gambling debts that he couldn't pay off. There'd been no sacrifice in his actions. Only weakness. And his pain, however deep it had been, hadn't disappeared with his death. He'd simply passed it on to those who'd loved him.

That's what really got to Emerson.

The selfishness of it all.

And yet . . .

And yet the Mustang was a car that no one in the surviving Tate family could bear to get rid of. The thought of seeing someone else cruising through town in it, filling it with their own life, their own memories, when all they had was their grief and their bitterness, was unfathomable. So Emerson's mom had kept the car, driving it only once when they lost the house on Outlook and were forced into the apartment complex. Over the years, she'd kept it covered, if not serviced, and for that Emerson was grateful. When he'd turned sixteen and gotten his provisional license, he'd gone to her and asked for the key.

She'd cried. She always cried.

"You look like him," she said. "Oh, baby."

Emerson had clenched his jaw, had strained to hold his own sorrow at bay. She'd been through so much over the years, not only as a widow, but as a mother accused of terrible, terrible things, the worst. "I know."

Then she'd given him the key, kissed him on the cheek, and made him promise to drive his brother around. Emerson was fine with that, but Miles never needed a ride anywhere and it was strange how not needing something could feel like a rejection.

Even stranger, though, was how, at this very moment, this car with its echoes of death and decisions and life courses forever altered was the one place where Emerson had never felt so vividly *alive*. The top was down, he was curling through the valley up toward Calistoga and May was riding in the passenger seat beside him. She had her sandals off, feet tucked beneath her.

A smile on her lips.

Having her with him, so close and so perfect, was pure September bliss.

Emerson stuck his arm into the breeze and grinned. Morbid, yes, but maybe that meant he could touch heaven from here.

*This is not a date,* he reminded himself as he held open the front door to the high-end creamery, which was the place May had suggested they stop for food. *This is definitely not a date.*

A brass bell tinkled overhead as they entered. And it really wasn't. A date. This was a class project, plain and simple, the same one everyone else in their Research Methods class had been assigned to complete: a visit to Calistoga's Petrified Forest to gather information on carbon dating. Still, Emerson liked to think that he and May being partners meant something. They could've chosen other people, after all.

Emerson took the shopping-for-food thing as another positive sign: she wanted to eat with him. He watched as May strolled the store's narrow aisles, dragging her feet along the scuffed wood floor, humming under her breath and picking out things like organic cheese and meat and buttery, warm bread and even homemade ice cream with bourbon and cornflakes in it. Emerson loved the way the food smelled and he loved the idea of them picnicking together in the grass, but he felt a sick twinge of guilt over the amount of money he was about to spend. Why was it the simplest foods always cost the most? Another guilt pinch came from the knowledge that Miles couldn't eat anything here. Well, maybe the meat, but surely even that had been cured or smoked or treated in some way his brother's nervous system couldn't tolerate. Then of course, thinking of Miles led to even more bad feelings. *Damn.*

That kid.

May turned around then. It was like she could read his mind. "How's your brother?" she asked. The wire basket filled with their food swung from her arm like a metronome.

*Tick tock.*

Emerson shrugged. "He's all right."

"Yeah?"

"Yeah."

"People are saying he's crazy."

"He's not crazy."

"Well, they say he talks to himself and stuff."

"Maybe he does. I don't know. Kid's been sick his whole life. He's probably lonely. He probably needs someone to talk to."

"Mmm," May said as she drifted toward the cash register. "Isn't that what a big brother is for?"

The Petrified Forest was part tourist trap, part natural wonder. Tucked away in a town known for its hot springs and mud baths sat this vast sloping park that featured hikes through groves of petrified redwood trees estimated to be over three million years old. According to the pamphlets the park owners handed out—only after the admission was paid, of course—a volcanic explosion was the cause of the petrification, a great magma burst freezing the giants like gods on a mountain and preserving them through the ages so that one day high school students could wander in pairs among the ferns and collect information with which to complete their class projects.

Emerson parked the Mustang at the foot of a mossy oak tree and left the top down because the day was just that damn nice. He and May set about gathering up the food, their notebooks, pens, jamming everything into bags. May had a smartphone, too, so they could take pictures for their presentation, which would've been cool if only it didn't make Emerson feel crappy about his own not-so-smart phone, which was the only thing he could afford.

Crossing the gravel lot on their way to the main gate, they passed a handful of cars. Lots of SUVs, some out-of-state ones, and a few vehicles Emerson thought he recognized from school. Including a shiny black Jetta with a familiar bumper sticker on the back window. Black lettering on the logo. An *S* and a *V* intertwined. Su Vin.

His throat went dry. Was that car *Sadie's*?

"What's wrong?" May was staring at him, brown eyes wide with concern.

Emerson blinked. Shook his head. "Nothing's wrong."

He walked forward on stiff legs, and May followed. She didn't ask any more questions and when they got inside and began the tour through the trees, Emerson longed to take her hand. Bump his hip against hers. Return her flirting looks and soft, dreamy gazes.

But he didn't.

*God.*

What was wrong with him? The moment was perfect and he was choking. Emerson had dated girls before, nothing serious, but he was no virgin. A senior girl had taken care of that when he was fifteen—a queasy one-off rutting in the bushes outside a postgame party that found Emerson too drunk or nervous to finish. It still put him ahead of a lot of guys, though, including Miles, who, at fifteen, didn't even know sex existed. So there was no excuse for not chasing what his heart desired. Was it because May was black and he wasn't, and they were out in public? Was he worried what other people might think? Or was it more than that? Sadie's words from when they'd run into each other the other day had wounded him deeply. Worse, they'd gotten stuck inside his head like a crappy pop song set on repeat.

*So you like niggers now?*

*I remember how you used to talk about them.*

Emerson cringed, embarrassed on his own behalf. More than embarrassed, he was mortified. But he'd changed since then, of course. He didn't use ignorant words or say hateful things. Not anymore. Race wasn't even something he thought about these days, because that's what you were supposed to do. Pretend it didn't matter.

Still, maybe he was worried about Sadie, knowing she could be here, lurking in the shadows or around the next trail bend. The way she'd looked at him in the school hallway hadn't been nice, sharp eyes sizing him up like a challenge. In fact, nothing he knew of Sadie was nice. But the worst part was, Emerson knew *he* hadn't been nice when they'd known each other. That's how they'd become friends, after all. Through simple sadism.

His own.

Right after their father's death, when his mother had worked as a hospice care nurse for Sadie's dying grandfather and couldn't afford a sitter, Emerson and Miles had been allowed to roam the Su winery when they got out of school. Miles was little and pitiful then, wouldn't leave their mother's side, but Emerson had been different. Impulsive. Imperious. The new man of the house. Nine-year-old Sadie caught him pulling legs off a tree frog he'd found on the edge of the vineyard near the boggy creek that ran north to south through the property.

"So you're like that," she'd called to him from the tree branch where she perched high in the air and spied on him.

Emerson had leapt back and looked up, face burning with shame and righteousness. At his feet, the dying frog lay splayed out on the ground, its tiny detached legs coated in dust like they'd been rolled in Cajun rub or something meant to flavor them.

"I'm like what?" he'd retorted.

Sadie wriggled farther down the tree branch so that she was closer, but not so close that he could reach her. She wore pigtails and a Catholic school uniform.

"Bad," she told him. "You're a bad person."

"Shut up. No, I'm not. You don't know me."

"I don't need to know you. But don't look so pissed off. Nothing's wrong with being bad. It's like being honest or crying at the end of a sad movie. Sometimes it just happens."

Now, almost a decade later, as he walked through the Petrified Forest, it hurt Emerson to remember those moments, which were more his failures than Sadie's.

But maybe that's what kept him from telling May his true feelings, from reaching out and touching her or letting her touch him. It wasn't Sadie or society or other people that held him back. It was himself. His own guilty conscience.

Maybe he still believed what that little girl had told him all those years ago.

# *chapter six*

"I need you to sign some papers," Sadie said when she sat down to dinner. It was mid-September, a school night, and already the breeze from the veranda had turned chill and the air ripe with the scent of crush season. Autumn was here.

"I need you not to tell me what to do," her mom volleyed back.

Sadie didn't answer, and they got halfway through their meal—Sadie wolfing down a hanger steak, plate swirling with blood; her mother, gin and vermouth—before words were spoken again.

"You going to class?"

Sadie nodded.

"You'd better be. I'm still paying that kid's medical bills, you know."

"I just said I was."

"Prove it, then. Tell me what're you learning."

"The art of war."

"What?"

"Fencing," Sadie said, and now her attention was starting to wander. From the table to the stars twinkling outside, bright dots in the vast valley sky. There were so many things she and her mother didn't talk about. Like where her father was, and if he'd ever come back. Like whether Sadie admired or hated him for leaving in the first place.

The phone in her pocket buzzed but Sadie knew better than to pull it out. It must be a text. From Wilderness Camp Chad probably. Turned out he lived in nearby Petaluma. He'd started up with her over the weekend.

*I'm home now. Wanna see you.*
*Send me yr tits. I'm lonely.*
*I'm not far. I can come to you. I gotta car. I'll drive.*
*Where u at girl? Don't be a bitch.*

That last one had made Sadie smile. Had she ever been anything but a bitch to him? That had not been her intent.

"Sadie!" her mom snapped. It was the type of tone that would've startled Sadie if she were the type of person who got startled. But she wasn't. So she looked up. Let her hair fall slowly into her face.

"Yes?" she said.

Her mother, who was pretty and blond and Dutch milkmaid soft on the outside, but ill-tempered polecat on the inside, was not fooled. She could read an adolescent fuck-you like nobody's business. "You're not on drugs, are you?"

"Alcohol's a drug, Mom. We live on a drug farm."

"Don't start with the drug farm thing."

"We're practically terrorists."

"Jesus, Sadie. I just want you to graduate. That's all."

"Well, wants aren't needs, you know."

Her mother snorted. "Oh, please. You're the one who said you needed me to sign something in the first place."

Sadie took her fork and stabbed at her steak remnants until juice splattered onto the tablecloth. "I have to see the school psychologist or else I'll get kicked out. And until I'm eighteen you gotta say it's okay."

"What psychologist?"

"I don't know. His name's MacDougall or something. Maybe he's Scottish."

"It's a guy?"

"It's a guy."

"Whatever. Fine. I'll sign the papers. But you'd better not tell him anything bad about me. Talk about your own problems."

"It's therapy. I'm supposed to be honest."

Sadie's mother sat back and laughed. "Yeah? Good luck with that."

Sadie slipped from the house after dinner. For a cigarette.

For her sanity.

No one noticed. Gerald Corning, who managed the winery Sadie's mother still liked to say was hers, showed up and even more drinks were being poured in the Su household. They'd probably be up all night if her mother's low-cut dress and pushup bra were any indication. These kinds of things went both ways and Sadie could definitely read an adult fuck-you when she saw one. Her mother didn't care about fidelity or Sadie's father. In fact, she loathed him. She always had. It was no wonder he'd left.

But did that mean he didn't care about Sadie?

Out in the cool autumn night, feet crunching on gravel, a blackness settled in her chest. One that wasn't nicotine, but still felt dirty. Sadie was pretty sure she didn't feel things like tenderness or love or compassion. At least, not the way other people did. Sure, she loved it when she got her way or when other people left her the hell alone, but she didn't think that was the definition you were going to find in the pages of Merriam-Webster or anything.

But the few moments in her life that she could describe herself as being *at peace* had all occurred in the presence of her father. Just brief moments, mostly during times they'd traveled together. His work took him all over the world and she'd last seen him seven months earlier, in Helsinki, a post-boarding-school-expulsion trip that Sadie spent flu-struck and feverish, huddled in their hotel room, trying not to die. When she was twelve, however, she'd gone with him back to China, his home country. Over a span of ten days they'd explored the bustling streets of Beijing and Tianjin, before moving south to Ningbo. There they'd ambled along the coast and made their way into the steep-pitched mountains, staying overnight in a forest where hot water bubbled up from the earth and the air smelled of licorice. Her father, Sadie had realized somewhere on that trip, was not a happy person. But he wasn't trying to be happy and his not trying meant he wasn't dissatisfied. At the time, this insight had pleased Sadie.

It had made sense.

Not too many things made sense to her anymore, though. Maybe that's what her therapist would try and fix. Get her to be content with her discontent and not work so damn hard to make other people miserable just because she was bored. But in truth, being alone with her boring discontent sounded like a pretty shitty time, which was the reason she planned on driving Emerson Tate a little crazy now that he thought he was better than her.

It was the reason she did a lot of things.

Sadie wandered out to the main road and waited for cars to pass so that she could throw rocks at them. Ten minutes later no cars had passed, and she walked back up the drive to get her own Jetta. Once behind the wheel, she cut a left onto the two-lane highway and hit the gas. She drove due east and kept going and going until she reached a brand-new soccer facility that had been built during her absence. Fancy high-priced leagues played there. People who were too good to play at the high school or one of the local parks. People who believed grass could be a status symbol.

Sadie parked on the side of the road and got out. The fields were deserted this time of night. A cyclone fence ringed the property, but Sadie found a gate on the far side that had been left unlocked. She slipped in and cruised around. A mesh bag of soccer balls sat unattended near one of the goal posts, and Sadie dragged the bag back with her through the open gate, down a steep embankment, right to the muddy edge of the town river. A late season algae bloom made the cool black current reek of rotten eggs and dog farts.

Cigarette clenched between her lips and using the long blade of the jackknife she carried in her pocket, Sadie set about popping the balls one by one. Then she tossed them into the water. They bobbed away sadly, like the end of a minor tragedy.

Brow sweating, chest heaving with exertion, she sat her butt down in the muck and longed for something else to destroy. The phone in her pocket vibrated again and this time Sadie pulled it out, exasperated sigh already building in her lungs in anticipation of whatever nasty thing Wilderness Camp Chad might say in order to get her to go out with him.

But the message wasn't from Chad. Nor was the one before it. They were both from Roman Bender. Emails, since Roman refused to own a cell phone and wouldn't text for reasons Sadie had never understood.

The first one read:

Hey. It's me. I don't want trouble.

Then maybe that poor kid whose life she'd fucked up so badly had waited for her to respond or else he'd simply struggled to come up with the right words, because his second email, sent a full forty-five minutes later, read:

> I just want to know why you did it.
>
> Please.

# *chapter seven*

Fencing class blues.

Miles had them.

The girl who'd somehow become his sparring partner lunged forward and hit him again and again. Miles stood stoically in defeat. Or what he thought was stoically.

The girl yanked her helmet off in disgust. "You're not even trying."

"How do you know that?" Miles asked. "How do you know I'm not trying? Maybe this is the best I can do."

"You don't move."

Miles removed his own helmet and laid it gently on the floor beside his foil. "I need water."

The girl trailed after him, too close for his comfort. She was small, smaller than him, and wore her sweaty hair pulled back in a ponytail. Despite their default pairing, Miles didn't know her name and didn't intend to ask. What he did intend to do was shrink as far away as possible from her as they walked. He wanted to make sure they didn't accidentally touch.

She piped up again while he was bent over the water fountain. "I saw you puking behind the Dumpster at 7-11 this morning."

He turned to glare at her.

She batted her eyes and smiled. Her cheeks had dimples. "I've seen you do it before, you know. You use a plastic bag. It's cute."

He stood up straight. "I have food allergies."

"Is that what you call a hangover these days?"

"I'm not hung over," he said. "I've never been hung over in my life."

"Really? After that crazy thing you did last week, wandering around like a nut, talking to the sky, I thought you were pretty wasted. You should see a doctor about your allergies then. Find out what makes you sick."

"I know what makes me sick."

The girl cocked her head. "Then why do you keep eating it?"

"Go away," Miles mumbled. "I don't want to talk to you."

The girl shrugged, then obliged. Miles felt weird, not inside his head, but all over, like the world around him was spinning at some strange new speed and his body had yet to acclimate. He asked the PE teacher if he could run laps for the rest of the period instead of dueling. The teacher nodded and waved him off. Miles wriggled out of his uniform and left it folded neatly by his locker. Then he went outside.

Once on the track, Miles started to jog. He'd had the weird feeling for days now, ever since the vision, the one he knew was coming but couldn't see clearly. His visions always came true, and they always ended with death. He remembered his first vividly: in the aching months after his father's suicide, a flock of headless crows had haunted his childhood dreams, well before he'd seen the birds in real life.

Since then his visions had snowballed, growing bigger, more powerful, as if his own grief were a conduit for more. By now Miles had seen it all, gripping flashes of the future that predicted car accidents and natural disasters, murder and mass suffering, even that bombing at the Boston Marathon and the Japanese tsunami. But this recent vision confused him. Miles thought this was because it involved *him* somehow. That hadn't happened before, and he didn't know what to make of it, didn't know if it meant he was doomed or saved. What he *did* know, however, was dire: the clock was ticking, and the countdown had begun. He had days, weeks, maybe a month. Miles knew he needed to understand, but then again, his needs never amounted to much.

Miles tried moving a little faster. He increased his stride and pumped his arms. The running felt good, an act that quieted his mind, although his shoes were worn thin and the jean shorts chafed his thighs raw. A group of guys were playing Frisbee near the south end of the track. They stopped to watch him pass.

"Hey, fag!" one of them called out cheerily.

# *chapter eight*

Emerson balked at Trey's suggestion. He put his head down and dribbled out to half court. No, he didn't want to go to Trish Reed's house on Friday night. That was the last thing he wanted to do. He also didn't want to talk about it.

What Emerson *did* want was to keep shooting hoops all afternoon at his favorite city park. Located smack in the center of Sonoma, it was a place where he could enjoy patches of warm sun and heated moments of sweat-soaked glory. It was a place where chickens ran loose in the grass. Then, after he was done playing ball, Emerson wanted to go home. Take a shower. Do his homework. Go to bed.

That was it.

Trey had a different idea, though, and so did his girlfriend Giovanna, who sat on a park bench in the shade, staring at her phone with obvious impatience. Emerson didn't care. They could go wherever the hell they wanted tomorrow night. He wasn't going to be a third wheel and he wasn't going someplace he didn't feel comfortable. In a school with two thousand students, he should be able to avoid one person without it being a big deal. That seemed fair. Reasonable.

Especially when that person was Trish Reed.

Blowing air through his cheeks, Emerson whirled around, bent his legs, and took a three-point shot. Terrible. His form was terrible. The ball banked off the rim. Trey went in for the easy rebound, then circled back to make a layup.

Emerson hung his head.

"C'mon, man," Trey said to him, dropping the ball and letting it roll into the grass. "You gotta go. Once the season starts, our Friday nights'll be gone. Poof. It's now or never."

Emerson glanced at Giovanna. "Parties are more fun when you've got someone to go with."

"You're kidding, right?"

Sweat rolled down Emerson's forehead, dripped off his nose. "Will May be there?"

"Dunno," Trey said. "And hell, just ask her out or something, all right? Her shit stinks, too, you know."

"Fuck," Emerson said. "Jesus, man. Don't talk like that."

"What I mean is, you don't go for it, someone else will. Someone who's not worried about having his perfect fantasy ruined by reality."

"I'm not worried about that. It's just, I like her."

"That's what I mean. You've been friends for years. You've always *liked* her. But now you want to screw her, and it's messing with your head. But she's still the same girl. She's still cool."

"Yeah, yeah." Emerson swiped at his face with his arm. He felt tired now, like maybe he just wanted to go home and be done with the day. Be done with everything. He wasn't even sure how they'd gotten onto the topic of May, because it wasn't May he was thinking about. It was Trish. Well, her and her DA father. That family-wrecking asshole. Worse even, seeing as he was the kind of asshole willing to go after families that had already been wrecked.

"Hey." Trey said in a conspiratorial tone, cocking his head in Giovanna's direction. "Think you can drive us to her house? Her folks are out of town."

Emerson trotted over to retrieve the basketball. "Why not? Might as well get you laid."

*Why not* made its case in no time. Things went from bad to worse on the drive out to Giovanna's. She lived outside of town, in the country, and on the way they passed the new soccer facility, where a single patrol car sat in the parking lot. No siren, but the lights were flashing. Emerson made sure to stay well below the speed limit.

Trey grinned and punched his arm when he saw the cop. "'Bout time they hassled some rich folks for a change, huh?"

Emerson wanted to grin back because he and Trey would never be rich folks. They would never play on a club league that charged twenty grand a year in dues and groomed kids to snag scholarship spots that cost less than what their parents paid for them. But Emerson didn't feel the urge to bond over poverty at the moment. That's because up ahead, walking on the shoulder of the highway, was his own brother.

*Shit.*

He slowed the car down.

Giovanna leaned forward. "Hey, is that Miles?"

"Yeah."

"He looks like a *hobo*."

Emerson couldn't really argue with that, but he wasn't sure who the sudden rush of anger he felt was directed at. Giovanna? Miles? He honked the horn. Got Trey to roll down his window.

"Hey!" Emerson shouted. "What are you doing?"

Miles jumped like a jackrabbit, then stared at them with his usual haunted, deer-in-the-headlights gaze. His hair was an oily mess.

"I'm walking," he said finally.

"Well, get in. You don't have to walk."

"I'm okay."

"You're in the middle of nowhere."

"I'm okay with that, too."

"Fine." Emerson bit his tongue. He had a way of getting frustrated with Miles that wasn't healthy for either of them. "See you later."

He pulled back onto the highway and kept going. Cranked the radio up because he didn't want to hear any commentary at his brother's expense. Emerson's head was still cloudy with ire when he turned down the narrow lane where Giovanna lived. A rural spot with small houses, but a pretty road nonetheless, lined with swaying trees and neatly trimmed hedges. A flock of crows dotted the sky. Although *flock* wasn't the right word, was it? A group of crows was actually called a—

"Look out!" Trey shouted. Emerson hit the brakes, but it was too late. There was a screeching of tires, followed by a soft thud. The air reeked of hot rubber as they scrambled out of the car. A large tabby cat lay in the road with a broken neck and glassy eyes. It had a blue suede collar with a bell on.

Emerson swore. Giovanna clasped her hands to her face and started to cry.

A nightmare. This was a total nightmare. The cat wasn't Giovanna's, but a neighbor's, and Emerson knocked on their door, only they weren't home. He was forced to leave a scrawled note of apology on the back of Trey's fantasy football picks, which he knew made him look like a total tool, but it was the only paper he had. Then, using his bare hands, Emerson moved the dead cat to the shoulder beneath a eucalyptus tree so no one else would run over it.

A chill floated into the air like a warning. Giovanna sprinkled white honeysuckle flowers over the animal's striped fur. Trey said nothing, just looked shaken. They all stood there for a moment. Then, because there was nothing else for them to do, Emerson waved good-bye to his friends, got back into his car, and drove off. He glanced once in his rearview mirror, just in time to see the sun fall behind the hills and darkness creep up behind him.

*Yea, though I walk through the valley of the shadow of death,* Emerson thought wearily. Followed by: *I need a goddamn drink.*

# *chapter nine*

"Why don't we talk about why you're here?"

It was her first therapy session with him, and Dr. Call-Me-Tom MacDougall looked as shabby and unprepared as Sadie had feared. He had a baby face and very blue eyes, also like a baby. Sadie was inclined to be critical, but he sat in a chair that had wheels on the bottom, for God's sake. Not to mention the specks of his lunch that dotted his shirt and the fact that one of the oversized laces on his fashion sneakers was untied.

"I'd rather not," she told him in a rare moment of candor.

"Then what do you want to talk about?" He had a small laptop perched on his knees, fingers poised at the ready.

Sadie racked her brain. A part of her wanted to screw with him, make him flustered and red-faced, and wish her gone. She could do it, too. He was young, probably fresh out of therapy school, and it wouldn't even matter if he were gay or straight. She could talk about sex or masturbation, about the slick heat of female desire and how she sometimes woke with a lit match burn between her legs that drove her out of bed and into the world, ready to set fire to anyone or anything that got in her goddamn way.

She could definitely tell him all that.

And it would drive him crazy.

But Sadie resisted. She held her impulses in check for the greater good. Her good, that is. Dr. Call-Me-Tom had already given her some speech about how he might need to refer her to another doctor if he deemed her "issues" too far outside his area of expertise. That would be a pain in the ass, Sadie thought. The school probably wouldn't think too highly of it, either.

"I've seen therapists before, you know," she said. "Lots of them."

"I'm aware of that."

"Have you talked to them?"

His head bobbed like a toy. "Briefly. Your mother gave me permission to gather information that might be relevant to our work together."

*Her mother.* Sadie twitched, wondering what details of her life might've already been shared. The day she set fire to her parents' wedding photos, no doubt. Or how she'd gotten thrown out of preschool for "emotional cruelty." Maybe even the time the loud-mouthed neighbors had attempted to file a restraining order against her, because Sadie put maggots in the potato salad at their big Fourth of July celebration. "Tell me what's wrong with me then. From all the information gathering you've done."

Dr. Call-Me-Tom sat back in his chair. "I don't have a professional opinion yet. Maybe there's nothing wrong with you."

Sadie was skeptical. "You think?"

"Thinking isn't the same as knowing."

*Touché, Dr. CMT.*

"What *do* you know then?" she asked.

"I know that you have a history of acting out."

"Is that a technical term? Do I have, like, an Acting Out Disorder?"

"It's possible. When a child's acting out is more excessive or destructive than what's considered normal, we sometimes refer to their behavior as *oppositional defiant*. There's information in your history to support that diagnosis. However, for an older child or teenager who's established a pattern of destructive or antisocial behavior, the criteria is sometimes met for what we call a *conduct disorder.*"

God. He even sounded like a textbook. What was this *we* business? And had he called her *a child*? Sadie was sure this guy didn't get laid. Ever. "So then that's it, right? That's my deal? I mean, we both know I've done antisocial things. That kid at my last school, Roman. He almost died because of me. I know that's what you want to talk about."

"That is what I want to talk about. But I can't give you a diagnosis. Behavior is one thing. But there's still always . . ."

Sadie leaned forward. "Always what?"

"Context," he said.

Sadie told her new therapist a few other things, nothing critical, but what she didn't tell him was this: Roman Bender was on her mind of late. Ever since the night he'd emailed her, he'd occupied her dreams, her nightmares, her every waking moment. She hadn't replied, of course, but he had her attention. Wasn't that something? After all this time, he was finally doing something right.

It was almost four in the afternoon by the time her appointment was over, and the school was already empty. Sadie stalked off campus and got into her Jetta. She cruised aimlessly with the music up and her windows down before driving to that taqueria she liked that was located behind the train station. There, Sadie ordered a soda and two shredded chicken tacos with hot sauce. She took her food away from the picnic tables and neatly trimmed grass and wandered close to the train tracks. Settling herself on the flat surface of a large rock, she unwrapped her tacos, wadded up the waxy paper into a tight ball, and let the wind take it.

There wasn't much to see from here, which was what she wanted. She was chasing peace. But boredom soon set in, and Sadie kept noticing things that brought up her memories of him. She couldn't help it. The thick roll of fog coming over the hills from the west, chilling the valley and rustling through the trees, reminded her of those autumn hikes in the New York woods—gold-red-bronze leaves crunching underfoot, the air ripe with chimney smoke, and Roman trailing after her like a lost puppy, while she told him whatever the hell was on her mind.

A tall, serious boy, Roman had worn his hair military short like his Marine father, but the style never suited him. To Sadie, he'd looked like a shorn lamb, offered up for the lion. Especially with those desperate hangdog eyes of his. The ones that said he'd given up hoping anyone would ever believe in him but didn't know why. And he'd had so many questions for her. Real questions. About life. About death. Morality. Anything.

Things no one else ever asked Sadie about.

"There are two kinds of people in this world," she'd told him once. "People who can give the benefit of the doubt and people who can't.

Compassion's like a gift, you know? Think about it. Some people, they know it's your birthday, and they just want to rush out and pick out the perfect thing for you. They don't care what it costs. They don't care if it's silly or trendy or something they wouldn't like. They want to make you happy. Gift giving makes them feel good. Your happiness makes them feel good. It has meaning.

"Then there are those people who know it's your birthday. And they know they *should* get you something. But they don't ever get around to actually doing it. They'll say things like 'gifts are materialistic.' Or they didn't have enough time and it's the thought that counts. But those are all lies. The truth is, they don't care. Your happiness doesn't make them feel good, so there's no motivation to do it. It's the same thing with compassion. It's not something that's handed out freely. Most of us are looking for excuses not to give it."

# *chapter ten*

Friday morning, Miles awoke long before his brother did. It'd always been that way. Miles had looked it up online once and learned that Emerson was a *night owl.* By contrast, he was a *morning lark,* fueled by a rattling set of circadian rhythms and social zeitgebers that shook him from sleep hours before the sun rose.

Slick as a lake trout, he slipped from beneath the sheets to the worn carpet. Pills and frays shocked his bare knees while he fumbled around on the floor in the dark for clothing. Across the room Emerson lay snoring in his own bed, thanks to a deviated septum from a childhood fall that had occurred at the automotive shop where their father had worked.

Their dad had been stern with them back then, bringing the boys to his place of employment, telling them not to run around and climb on things. But Emerson hadn't listened because Emerson never listened, and when he'd gotten hurt it'd been no one's fault but his own. Years later, the grate of his subsequent snoring was a bleak reminder of both the accident and the fact that there'd never been money for surgery to fix the problem. Not when Miles was in and out of the emergency room as often as he was. He supposed Emerson resented him for this, draining the family bank account with illness and ailment and legal proceedings.

He supposed Emerson resented him for a lot of things.

Once inside the bathroom, Miles flipped on the light and the fan and locked the door. He balled his clothes up in the corner and opened the bottom drawer of the sink vanity. A black notebook and a bland assortment of pens lay inside. There were other items in the drawer, too, like ipecac, ephedrine, Imitrex, things he often needed to make himself feel better. Mind humming with urgency, Miles grabbed for the notebook and selected a slim black rollerball, the cheap kind from the drugstore that usually stained his fingers with ink.

He crouched with his back against the wall, thumbed quickly to a blank page, and began to draw. He sometimes did his sketching while seated on the toilet or else sprawled in the tub, head numbed by migraine as he leaned against cool yellow tile pockmarked with mold, cobwebs dangling in the corners above him. But today his body had none of its usual complaints or banal needs, and Miles soon lost himself in the act, tight fingers swirling-scrawling-scratching in an effort to re-create his dreams, those dark moments he believed to be echoes of his vision. He drew a river run red with blood. The glinting sun shining off the blade of a sword thrust upward into the air.

The grace and agony of his own stunning death.

Ripe with violence.

Steeped in shame.

# *chapter eleven*

"Where were you this morning?" a female voice asked.

"Huh?" Emerson set down the sandwich he was attempting to eat and squinted. It was lunch period, and he was sitting alone on a bench at the far edge of the school's main quad. Clouds floated in the sky above, casting haze, but the day was bright enough so that the girl speaking to him was completely backlit. All he could make out was the soft golden glow around her head. A solar halo.

"Where were you?" the girl asked again, twisting her body like a helix as she spoke. Then she flopped beside him with a sigh. Emerson's breath hitched inward. It was May in fall—pretty as a postcard and then some. She smiled warmly at him then leaned so close that one of her dusky plum-ripe breasts threatened to leap from her tank top and graze against Emerson's shoulder. But what should have felt like a gift, didn't. Dead leaves swirled in the wind. Numbness swirled through his veins.

Emerson shrugged listlessly. "Had to take my brother to the hospital."

"Is he okay?"

"No. I mean, yes. I mean, he'll be all right. But no, he's not okay. He never is."

She frowned. "What's wrong?"

*~what's wrong what's wrong what's wrong~*

A chill slithered up Emerson's spine. Those two words were the echo of his childhood. They were the ones whispered in hospital corridors, the ones spilled from the lips of social workers and lawyers. They embodied the existential mystery that was Miles.

"They're running tests," he said. "Could be a virus. Could be his allergies. Could be . . ."

"Could be what?" May asked.

"Anything." Emerson shuddered. The memory of breaking down the bathroom door that morning and finding his brother splayed out on the floor, his heartbeat tachy, left leg twitching, wearing nothing but a dingy pair of briefs with a torn waistband, was a moment he couldn't stop replaying in his mind. Their mother had been working graveyard out at the home in Napa, so Emerson was the one who'd called for an ambulance. Who'd ridden to the ER with Miles. But *what's wrong* wasn't what he'd shouted at his brother as he grabbed his shoulder and tried to shake him out of his seizing stupor. No, Emerson had demanded to know *what happened*?

Which was a different question altogether.

"He's sick a lot, isn't he?" May looped her arm through his. "You've mentioned that."

"Yes."

"Is it serious?"

"No," Emerson said. "That's the thing. He's sick a lot, but the doctors never find anything wrong."

"I don't understand."

Emerson grunted in response. Of course she didn't. May had moved to Sonoma their sophomore year. She hadn't been here when his family had been dragged through hell, landing first in the local paper, then the county courthouse. She didn't know how Gracie Tate's name had become linked to the cruelest sort of torture. The whole thing had unraveled after a string of hospitalizations when Miles was ten. Emerson grew five inches that same year, slamming into puberty like an ox, but even he couldn't stop his little brother from wilting into sad bouts of stomach pains and fever spikes. Eventually, a concerned hospital employee filed a CPS report, claiming there was a pattern to Miles's symptoms, one that indicated he was in urgent danger from the person trusted most to care for him. There was even a name for it, the report said: Munchausen syndrome by proxy. That's what it was called when doting mothers poisoned their children, injecting them with pus and feeding them actual shit, all so they could make their kids sick with the sole purpose of taking them to the hospital in order to be saved. *Their* mother had done no such thing, of course, but it turned out proving you weren't killing your own kid for attention wasn't so easy, even when you were innocent. It turned out some lies were so lurid everyone wanted to believe they were true.

"I don't understand it either," Emerson said.

May made a clucking noise of sympathy and brushed her cheek against his shoulder. She was practically nuzzling him now, her nose to his chin, and it seemed like she wanted him to reach out, wrap his arm around her, only Emerson didn't do that, because the closer May got, the closer that plum-ripe breast came to slipping right out into the open. It bulged from her shirt in a promising way, like a sea creature coming up for air, and Emerson stared. He couldn't do anything else. He thought if he shifted, just the tiniest bit, then the plum would be resting right in his palm. It was the perfect size for him to hold, the perfect shape for him to reach up with his thumb and forefinger and gently grasp its dark center—

"I have to go," he said, getting to his feet so quickly, May collapsed sideways like a house of cards.

She righted herself, but her expression was one of bewilderment. "What's the matter?"

He bent awkwardly, grabbing for his backpack and stuffing his uneaten lunch in with his books and papers. "I need to call the hospital." A lie, but Emerson didn't know what else to say. He couldn't sit here with her curled against him, fantasizing about grabbing her tits with his dick getting hard. Not with everything that was going on. Not when all this with Miles could be starting over again, and his mom might need him.

*Fuck,* he thought. *My fucking brother.*

May watched him closely. "Is there anything I can do?"

Emerson shook his head. Pulled his backpack over his shoulders. Ran fingers through his hair.

"I'm sorry," he said.

# *chapter twelve*

It was Friday night, and Chad showed up for his date with Sadie in a black Civic with tinted windows and a fishtail spoiler.

Of course he did.

Sadie's mother peered from the living-room window out to where both boy and car idled. The Honda was lit up by the glow of custom lighting that lined the circular drive and the strands of tiny white bulbs that twined around the massive oak gate leading out to the rest of the property—those sprawling acres that included gardens and grapevines and barrel halls and tasting rooms and even the type of underground cellar that held not just wine or roots but the deepest and darkest of secrets.

"Great choice," her mother said. "You sure know how to pick them."

Sadie bristled. "I met him at that place *you* sent me to."

"What place?"

"The wilderness camp. In Santa Cruz."

"Interesting. I thought I sent you to an all-girls camp."

This made Sadie smile her warmest smile. "You did."

"You'd better come home tonight," her mother warned. "I mean it."

Sadie didn't answer. Of course she planned on coming home, but no one needed to know that but her. She grabbed her coat and skipped from the house to where Chad stood waiting by the driver's-side door, his best bad-boy scowl punctuating his pimply face. Sadie skipped because her mother was watching, and she skipped because it meant she hadn't a care in the world.

She didn't, after all.

Care.

They went to the drive-in out by the community college. Across the road, a football game lit up the field, all Friday-night bright, the air humming with the crush of bodies and bones, the sweet-sick scent of violence.

A superhero film played on the screen. The men were muscular and bland, the women pale and spiteful, the whole plot nonexistent, but none of this stopped Chad from complaining loudly about the game and the noise and the light pollution while they sat on the hood of his car.

"Should be illegal to build a football stadium next to the drive-in," he growled.

Sadie ran her fingers over the car's glossy paint job in a swirling motion. Something raw pulsed beneath her rib cage, like her body was sending messages in Morse. She didn't mind the football game, and she really didn't get what Chad was going on about. Real violence was preferable to the fictional kind. Real violence told the truth, after all. "Maybe the stadium was here first."

Chad looked at her. "Was it?"

She shrugged. "How would I know?"

"I want to fool around," he said, reaching for her tits, and even though they were sitting there, right out in public, Sadie let him. He pinched and squeezed, and she waited, wondering if she would feel something. She did sometimes, her indifference building into want then greed. Other times, though, she just felt disgusted by the effort. Like now.

She swatted his hand away. "Not here."

"In the car then."

"Mmm," she told him, hopping to the ground. "I want to *do* something."

"Come on, babe . . . ," he whined, but Sadie reached and pulled him down with her and away from the car. Chad wasn't meek like Roman, but she still couldn't or wouldn't explain to him what it was that smoldered inside of her. He needed to fuck. She needed something else. It was like they spoke different languages. Together, they crept down the rows of vehicles, winding farther and farther from the screen. Wafts of pot smoke drifted from open windows. Chad slid a flask from his jacket pocket and drank from it.

When they reached the end of the narrow pathway that ran between the cars, Sadie stopped. The two of them huddled in the shadow of the snack bar, where the roar of the football game echoed off the cement wall, louder than ever. Sadie pulled out her American Spirits. Lit up.

"Those make your mouth taste shitty," Chad said.

"You want to taste my mouth?"

Chad grinned and groped her again. Sadie didn't push him away, but she didn't do any groping of her own. Instead she sat stone still as she watched people walking to and from the snack line. It wasn't crowded, but there was a constant stream—families, married couples, college students on dates. Not who Sadie was looking for.

Not what she needed.

Then Sadie saw someone who made her sit up jackrabbit straight. She jumped to her feet, yanking her shirt down and ignoring the way Chad's eyes flashed with frustration.

"Trey," she called out, and when he didn't answer, she said it louder: "Trey!"

He turned, swiveling his tall basketball body around. He looked right at her.

"I want to ask you a question."

Trey's jaw clenched, and Sadie did her best to put him at ease. She smiled as she walked toward him, tilting her head to one side, playing with her hair.

"Have you seen Emerson?" she asked.

Trey's gaze darted to where Chad sat sullenly on the ground, sucking down more of whatever disgusting booze he'd dumped inside that flask of his.

"What do you want with Emerson?" Trey snapped.

"I told you at that party. He's an old friend of mine. We go way back."

"He sure doesn't talk about you like you're a friend."

"Well, I bet I've known him longer than you have."

"Oh, yeah?"

"We met right after his dad killed himself in that Mustang. Fourth grade."

Trey's eyes widened at this.

"You didn't know?" Sadie asked.

"I knew about his dad. But not . . . not the car."

"It fucked him up good," she said. Understatement of the year, of course.

"His brother's in the hospital again," Trey said quickly. "He's always getting sick, you know?"

Brother? Sadie searched the depths of her brain until she conjured a faint image of a small boy who had looked nothing like Emerson, but she could remember nothing else about him. A ghost child. Barely there. Had barely mattered.

"Trey." A girl with curled hair and red lipstick came out of the snack bar then. She had a soda in one hand, and the look she gave Sadie held the compulsory female blend of fear and challenge. "Let's go. This movie sucks."

"Yeah, sure." Trey sounded relieved.

"Where're you going?" Sadie asked.

"He's not interested," the girl said, reaching to grab on to Trey's elbow and guide him away.

The smoldering need inside of Sadie flared hotter, higher. She spun to face Wilderness Camp Chad. He'd set the flask down on the asphalt and was now tracing the scars on his wrist with his index finger. Well, that was sad, Sadie thought, but not in a pitying way.

More like pathetic.

"Come on," she said. "We've found our plans for the night."

Chad glanced up. "Yeah? Where we going?"

Sadie waved at the retreating figures of Trey and his girl. "Wherever the hell they are."

## *chapter thirteen*

Miles was stuck in the belly of the beast. That's how hospitals always felt to him. Like he was actually inside a living creature, dwelling in its bowels or lodged in some drafty airway or circulatory vessel. It soothed him in a way, to be surrounded by such a tight sense of containment and security—that pulsing rhythm of cause and effect; the vital and haunting sounds of other people being kept alive.

"Miles."

He jolted and looked up from the chair where he was seated. A gray-haired woman stood in the doorway to his room. Her white coat told him she was a doctor, but she wasn't one he'd ever met before.

She took a step forward, nodding toward the window. "It's dark out there."

"Yes," he said, because this wasn't an observation but a fact. It was almost ten o'clock. Night had fallen. That meant visiting hours were over and Miles was alone.

Or he had been.

"What are you looking at?" she asked.

He shrugged. The answer was nothing and everything, but that wasn't such a comfortable thing for him to say.

"Do you think we could talk?"

"Who are you?"

She came closer and sat on the edge of the bed. She had brown skin and dark eyes, and her limbs were very thin. Miles could see straight through to her bones. They wrestled and pressed at her flesh when she moved. As if her parts craved freedom more than the harmony of the whole.

"I'm sorry," she said gently. "I should've introduced myself. I'm Dr. Sahota. The attending pediatrician tonight."

"The last doctor that was here said I could go home in the morning."

"I saw that in your chart. Do you want to go home?"

"I want to do what I'm supposed to."

"That's not what I asked."

Miles pulled his knees to his chest and hugged them. He knew that wasn't what she'd asked, but he didn't intend to answer what she had.

Dr. Sahota cleared her throat. "The chart also says that your mom was working when you got sick this morning."

"Yeah."

"So you were by yourself?"

"No, I wasn't by myself. My brother was home. He helped me."

"What's your brother's name?"

"Emerson."

"How old is Emerson?"

"Eighteen."

"He must have been scared."

"I don't know about that."

"Why?"

Miles considered this. "Because my brother is strong."

"Being strong doesn't necessarily mean not being scared."

Didn't it, though? Somewhere above them someone flushed a toilet or turned on a shower because a great whoosh of water suddenly tumbled through the pipes with a rattle, and to Miles it felt like a white dove of fear had awakened inside his chest. The dove fluttered and scratched and cooed against his rib cage, making it hard for him to breathe.

Dr. Sahota watched him closely. "Do you ever feel scared, Miles?"

The dove's wings beat faster, harder, stirring up his pulse, his nerves. His sick, wild thoughts. This doctor was clearly here because she believed something was wrong with him, something worse than the electricity in his brain or the chemicals in his blood, and for a moment Miles longed to open up, to tell her *everything*: about how he was always scared, every minute of every day. About how the hospital was the one place he felt safe from his fears, wedged as he was in these beast-belly walls. About how he liked the safety but didn't like the fact that he couldn't access his visions here. About how he worried the darkness he saw in those visions meant there was darkness inside him, too, but that in a way, he longed for darkness, because even he hated his own weakness sometimes.

But Miles knew if he said any of these things that Dr. Sahota would think differently of him. That she'd want to keep him here and ask more of him than he was willing to give. And then he wouldn't *know.* That was unthinkable. His visions, they were his for a reason.

And they were the only reason he had for living.

So Miles shook his head and hoped the nice doctor with the thin skin and moving bones couldn't see through to the sadness that welled inside him, like reluctant rain clouds gathering for a coming storm.

"I'm tired," he lied. "I want to go to bed."

She nodded, gave a tight smile. "Okay, then. Sleep well."

# *chapter fourteen*

Emerson stood barefoot in the musty first-floor laundry room of his apartment building as he pulled clothes from the overworked dryer and stuffed them into a plastic laundry basket. He was alone in his Friday-night mundanity. A caged lightbulb hung from the ceiling. The air smelled of hot lint and static.

When the dryer was empty, Emerson checked the floor for stray socks, then gathered the basket in both arms. He made his way into the darkness outside, walking along the edge of the crumbling parking lot and steering clear of the sagging carport. The stars were out, and a harvest moon hung low in the sky. It prowled close to the hilltops like a great amber beast hot on the heels of its unlucky prey.

Back inside the apartment, Emerson found his mother sleeping. She lay curled on the couch in gray sweats and slippers, with the television on. He glanced at the screen. It was one of those housewives shows. Emerson hated the people on those shows, what with their designer clothes and vapid lives, but he thought maybe he could understand why his mom liked to watch. No one on those shows ever worried about paying bills on time. Plus, they complained so damn much, they made it easy to forget your own problems.

He set the laundry basket down on the carpet near the window and pulled a faded quilt over his mother. Then he switched the floor lamp off, but left the television on. The noise would be a good distraction from the yelling that would start up once the neighbors got drunk enough to stumble home from the bar in a bad mood.

Emerson sat and ate soup in the kitchen. Cream of broccoli, a whole can. Without Miles, the atmosphere in the apartment felt lighter, less oppressive. Emerson hated that he felt that way, but then again, Emerson hated a lot of things about himself.

From his back pocket, his phone buzzed. He pulled it out and looked.

It was from May.

His heart fluttered like an uncaged animal. And all she'd typed was: *Hey.*

*Hey,* he typed back.

*How's your brother doing?*

*He's fine.*

*Still at the hospital?*

*Yeah. Home tomorrow. They're keeping him overnight out of "an abundance of caution." Caution runs out in the morning, I guess.*

*Well, I'm glad he's feeling better.*

*Me too. Look, I'm really sorry I left like that at lunch.*

*Don't be sorry. I get it.*

*I want to see you. Where are you?*

*Trish's. Come by. Trey just got here. Giovanna too.*

Jesus, Emerson thought. Trish's. Of course.

*I'm coming,* he typed impulsively, before sneaking a glance at his snoring mother, at her soft blond hair and delicate features that looked like Miles's.

*"Fuck,"* he said out loud.

The party was raging by the time he got there. The Reeds owned a huge swath of land out near the Glen Ellen border, not far from some of the area's fancy health spas. Lucky for the Reeds, their wealth also afforded privacy: their property butted up against a golf course to the north, miles of thick woods to the south. From where Emerson sat in his car, he could see straight down into their private valley—there were dozens of cars strewn haphazardly across the back field and rap music boomed from the house, loud enough to shake the Mustang's windows.

He parked on the shoulder of the main road. A risk: the car could be sideswiped or rear-ended by anyone flying around the hairpin turns, but the alternative was actually driving his father's Mustang down onto the Reed property. Something about that felt traitorous. Like he was setting up camp with the Confederacy.

Or joyriding into hell.

He got out of the car, locked it. Shoved his hands in the back pockets of his jeans and began the dark walk toward the main house. The music grew louder, and Emerson's head throbbed sickly.

May, he reminded himself. That's why he was here.

May, May, May.

She was his delicate turn of the ankle.

She was his ice slowly melting.

God, he wanted her.

*So bad.*

As he drew closer to the party, Emerson tried picturing himself as a Trojan horse, a creature on offense, filled with weapons of his own. He had to think of himself this way, as something bold and powerful, just to keep his feet moving. In truth, he had no weapons, no tricked-out horse, and walking into this party felt more like crawling into the walls of a brazen bull than anything strategic. All because Emerson hadn't forgotten what Trish Reed had done in seventh grade, only one day after her DA father had filed child abuse charges against his innocent mother. It was something he would never forget.

Or forgive.

"No wonder their dad killed himself," Trish had whispered to a group of attentive girls in the schoolyard on that warm spring day, just loud enough for Emerson to hear. Her green eyes had been wide with concern, but her low voice and flush cheeks betrayed the thrill of fresh gossip. "He probably knew what their mom was doing. I bet it drove him crazy. I bet that's why he did it."

Emerson's mind spun with rage. He'd stormed right over to her. "You don't know what the hell you're talking about!"

Trish folded her arms, lifted her chin. She was middle-school perfect, all clear skin and budding breasts, like a well-bred rose on the verge of her bloom. "I know your mom's in jail right now."

He'd blazed white-hot. "That's not what I mean! Take back what you said about my dad. It's not true!"

She'd faltered then, her haughtiness sliding into horror as she realized what she'd done. Trish said nothing more, but it was too late. The ugly truth about his father's death was written all over her pretty face. Everyone knew.

And finally, a full three years after the fact, Emerson did, too.

---

The crowd was impressive. No doubt about that. It looked like half the high school had shown up and then some. There was even a live band playing in the field, shadowy figures who stood in the tall grass with their guitar pedals and microphones, cranking out broken chords and broken lyrics, with their amps pointed straight toward town. Like they were begging for the cops to come. Like they were tempting fate.

Then again, who the hell was going to arrest DA Reed's daughter?

Using his elbows, Emerson made his way from the wide front porch to the back of the house, where tiki torches lit the night and topless girls splashed in a hot tub set beneath the branches of a towering redwood tree. Like wet gifts on Christmas morning. He craned his neck in every direction but couldn't see May.

Next he tried squeezing into the actual house by way of the game room, which was where a DJ was set up and people were dancing. Bad idea. It was too packed for him to even reach into his pocket for his phone. Smashed up against backs and shoulders, and wedged tight to a speaker, Emerson grew sweaty. Then queasy, like maybe he really was inside one of those brazen bulls, being slowly roasted from below. Someone tried shoving a beer in his hand, but he pushed it away.

Where *was* she?

"Take it!" the beer shover shouted, and Emerson was this close to knocking the drink to the ground when he realized Trey was the one holding it. He breathed a sigh of relief. Took the beer. Downed it.

"You seen May?" he asked.

"Huh?"

"May!" he shouted.

Trey pointed to a doorway directly behind Emerson. "In there."

"Yeah?"

"Yeah. Just did a shot with her. Girl's nuts tonight. Go get her."

"Thanks, man."

Trey gave him a thumbs-up. Danced off into the crowd.

Sure enough, May was right where Trey said she'd be. The room was an alcove off the kitchen and she stood at a marble island, playing quarters with the rest of the girls from the volleyball team. And not very well. Something in the way she leaned and swayed told Emerson she'd probably had more than her fair share of alcohol tonight. Southern Comfort, from the looks of it.

She also took his breath away. May wore a dress that was gauzy and pale, with fabric so thin he could see straight through to her legs, her hips, her ethereal softness. She was so beautiful an actual moan escaped Emerson's lips, leaving him torn between wonder and lust, as if he might either weep with joy from being in her presence or else walk over, lift that dress up, and have his way with her, right there in the kitchen, in front of God and everybody.

But then, like the day they'd shopped together in the creamery and she'd asked about his brother, it seemed May could actually read his mind, because right as the most forbidden of thoughts bubbled into Emerson's consciousness, she turned.

And she saw him.

He blushed. Held up a hand in a shy wave of greeting.

What happened next was like a dream. Or a movie. She bounded for him, falling straight into his arms, her body warming him in the best and realest of ways. All around them, people whistled, laughed.

May looked right into his eyes and smiled.

*"You,"* she said.

## *chapter fifteen*

Sadie watched Emerson from across the room. She stood with her back against the kitchen wall, shoulders pinned to plaster, plastic cup of tepid beer held in one hand. A steady stream of huge guys and skinny girls pushed past her, but Sadie's attention was homed in on Emerson Tate and the long willowy black girl who had her hands all over him. Sadie hadn't expected to see Emerson after hearing about his brother and the hospital. But now that he was here, she couldn't take her eyes off him.

Not even if she wanted to.

The girl he was with was wasted. Beyond wasted: she was a sloppy mess. Sadie could see that the same way she could see male-patterned baldness and a future of divorce and despondency in the asshole who'd just spilled his drink on her good jeans. There were about fifteen shots written in the way the girl's legs twisted around themselves. Emerson tried holding her up, while at the same time tugging her skirt down. The girl writhed away from him once, throwing her arms in the air and dancing to the music beneath the spinning beam of a projected disco ball. She had no bra on, and her giant breasts shuddered and shook with each flail of her body. To Sadie they looked like flying udders, which was to say, gross, but the straight guys in the room clearly disagreed with this assessment. They stopped to gawk. And point.

Emerson reached to grab her, to stem the tide of spectacle. The girl grinned, put both hands on his cheeks, and kissed him hard. Sadie stood on her tiptoes, straining to see more. Emerson was kissing the girl back, but his eyes were open and he had one hand on her side and had begun walking backward, dragging her with him.

A loud crash came from outside, followed by yelling. The crowd's focus shifted, people turning midstride and heading for the French doors that led out to the backyard. There was more yelling, but over the music, Sadie couldn't tell if it was happy yelling, like cheering, or the sound of a witch hunt starting up. Chad better not be involved in anything untoward. She'd abandoned his drunk ass on the patio near the keg and a game of beer pong, and Sadie didn't *think* he'd do anything too stupid, like get into a fight or hit on the wrong girl. Chad was more likely to be the kid puking his guts up in the rose garden or caught dry humping pool toys at the end of a party.

That's what she hoped, anyway.

Someone backed into her then, smashing her foot and sloshing her drink onto the floor.

*Goddamn* it.

"Sorry," a gruff voice said, and Sadie's head snapped up, because it was Emerson talking to her. She said nothing, just stared at him, at his blond hair and handsome jaw. He didn't say anything else or even seem to realize who she was. He just kept walking, dragging the drunk girl with him. They headed toward a staircase that had a string across it, along with a neatly handwritten sign with the message DO NOT FUCKING GO UPSTAIRS penned on it.

As he read the words, Sadie saw determination set in Emerson's eyes. Or was it hunger? She couldn't tell.

Then she watched as Emerson ducked beneath the string, carried the girl up the stairs.

And vanished.

Sadie waited a few minutes before following. Patience was one of her few virtues, and she bided her time standing against the kitchen wall, staring at a predictably provincial rooster clock on the other side of the room, watching the minutes go by. She waited until even more high school students showed up, flooding the space with a rising tide of high fives and chest bumps. She waited until a bottle of crème de menthe was knocked to the floor and no one did anything about it, just tracked mint-flavored stickiness all over the damn place. She waited until no one remembered the drunk girl who'd tried to pull her dress up over her head or the guy who'd kept her from flashing her business to the entire party.

Of course, Sadie understood Emerson hadn't been acting out of *kindness* when he'd pulled the girl's dress down. He was a guy, after all, and guys liked to believe in some bizarre fantasy world where girls didn't think about or have sex—unless it was with them. As if the human achievement of populating the earth with seven billion people hadn't let that cat out of the bag. Then again, Sadie was familiar with a few of Emerson Tate's *other* fantasies. She highly doubted the willowy girl would go anywhere with him if she possessed the ability to see into his past.

When the moment was right, Sadie walked to the stairwell and stepped over the string and the sign with an air of pure confidence. She wasn't acting, either. It was confidence she actually felt. And it worked: no one stopped her or said a dissenting word.

She padded up the steps on quiet feet.

The home's second story was opulent and dimly lit: a long corridor of wide-planked flooring ornamented with plush runners and flickering copper sconces. With one ear cocked back to the stairwell, Sadie sidestepped her way down the hall, peeking into every room. She expected to catch all sorts of couples going at it, horny girls shaking off their bras, horny boys trying to shove their hands into honey pots.

But there was no one. Weird. Whoever's house this was must be mean as hell or else a card-carrying NRA member, since everyone here seemed driven by the same self-absorbed ruttiness that ensured babies would be made in the backs of cars and off-limits bedrooms at high school parties for all eternity. Like the pull of the tides, Sadie knew, no one was immune to longing like that, not even the shy, self-doubting kids, the ones who would never make a move or do anything but cry themselves to sleep over their failings and inadequacies. They probably wanted it more than anybody. Maybe it was because they knew how distant their dreams were from reality.

Maybe that's what made them so easy to hurt.

Sadie remembered the first time she'd stepped foot into Roman Bender's dorm room at their boarding school. How she'd looked around, taking in the whole space, the whole of who Roman was. What she'd seen there reminded her of her father during their trip to China. A certain bleakness. A distinct sort of misery.

The inside of his room had been ascetic and grim. Roman read

Camus. He played acoustic guitar. He was both dutiful and predictable in his depression. Even his bed sheets were drab—musty and stained with unwashed desire. Worse, Sadie could tell by the uncomfortable way he sat squirming at his desk that he was probably hard right then and there, simply by being in her presence. Nature was cruel like that, swelling his body with hope and possibility, when surely even his own mind knew better.

How could she want a boy like him when he needed *so much*?

"I'm not good enough for you," she'd told him briskly, both because it was true and because she thought it was a kind thing to say. Sadie wasn't used to being kind and, well, clearly she'd blown it, because Roman hadn't answered her at all. He'd just cleared his throat, once, twice, a third time, then stared at his shoes and the bare wood floor with his hangdog eyes.

Standing there, in the wake of his self-loathing, Sadie grew bored. Her attention drifted toward the window, to the world beyond. Outside on the campus lawn, every object shone and shimmered in the New York sun, vivid and alive. A dog barked. The trees were in color. Boys in varsity jackets tossed a football around, and girls with perfect bodies did cartwheels in the grass. But the dreadful silence inside that dorm room stretched and stretched, until Sadie couldn't stand it any longer. Roman wasn't vivid, but he was alive, and she decided right then and there that if her efforts at kindness weren't enough to keep him from falling further in love with her, she'd have to do it another way.

Her way.

A strange noise snapped Sadie back to the present. She frowned. Was that the sound of someone *crying*? Whatever it was, it had come from behind a closed door farther down the hallway. Sadie crept forward, pressed her ear to the keyhole, and listened.

It was a bathroom. It had to be. She heard water running.

Then whimpering.

And coughing.

Sadie wrinkled her nose. Ew. It sounded like that willowy girl was yakking up her night's worth of drinking. And then some.

There was more whimpering. Then a soft male voice.

"You okay?" That had to be Emerson. He sounded both brusque and weary.

There was no answer.

"You want me to take you home?"

Still no answer.

"May?"

Silence.

Sadie crouched by the door for what felt like an eternity, waiting to hear something, anything: more puking, someone taking a cold shower, Emerson snarling at the drunk girl to get her shit together. But there was nothing, and Sadie crouched there for so long she began to wonder if they'd left the bathroom through another door and moved into a different room. A yellow sliver of light sliced the space between the door and the floorboards, and she sprawled on her stomach, straining to get a glimpse inside.

She saw nothing.

She waited longer. More minutes ticked by until Sadie's patience came to its inevitable end. She *had* to know what was going on in there. Her body hummed with anticipation.

She reached up and grabbed the doorknob.

The heavy wood door creaked open, very slowly.

At first Sadie wasn't sure what she was seeing. It took a moment for her mind to catch up, and she noticed the parts before the whole: the willowy girl who wore nothing but her underwear and lay passed out on the white tile floor, bare brown tits pointing straight toward the ceiling, her face slack, and her eyes closed. Her gauzy puke-stained dress had been rinsed out and lay draped over the edge of a clawfoot tub, water dripping from its hem to the floor. And finally, Emerson himself, who sat on the very edge of the toilet with his pants around his ankles. He was gazing down at the girl with the funniest look on his face, and he wasn't touching her, not exactly, but he was doing *something,* and to see what it was brought a smile to Sadie's lips. In fact, she stood straight up and grinned ear to ear, like a fox with a full belly licking its paws after a hard kill.

Well, well, she thought.

Emerson Tate hadn't changed at all.

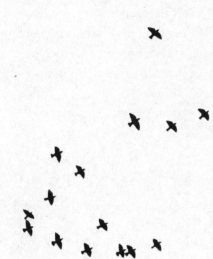

# *part 2*

## Little Lamb

Isaac spoke to Abraham his father and said, "My father!" And he said, "Here I am, my son." And he said, "Behold, the fire and the wood, but where is the lamb for the burnt offering?"

—Genesis 22:7

# *chapter sixteen*

"Get over here and suck me, girl."

"Squirrelly little shit."

These were the words that greeted Miles when he got to school Monday morning, which were then followed by jeering laughter. Not his. Naturally, the invitation was one he declined—or more accurately, ignored—and Miles made a mental note to avoid the west side entrance to Sonoma High until the end of time. This was in addition to the other places on campus he was loath to go, like the third-floor bathrooms, the school library, and any area that wasn't well lit or well populated. There was a terrible injustice, he thought, in being an introvert who was afraid of being alone.

Miles dragged himself to fencing class out of obligation more than anything. It's where his vision had first shown up, after all, and it's where he yearned to see more. No matter how wretched the future might be, the need to know it burned inside him like a hot candle on a cold night.

And it couldn't be worse than his present.

"You weren't here on Friday." The PE teacher didn't bother looking at Miles when he spoke to him. He just stood there in the gym with an oversized Styrofoam cup of coffee gripped in one hand and stared at the clipboard he held in the other. As if it were the one more likely to come up with an adequate response.

"I was sick," Miles said softly. And while he was safe from harassment in here, in this space, he still felt meek, a little flushed, a little out of sorts. Even his stomach rang hollow, despite having eaten breakfast, and everything around him felt so *bright*. An assault of the senses.

"You gotta note?" the teacher asked.

"No."

"Gotta have a note from your doctor or the absence is unexcused."

"Okay."

The teacher glanced up at him then. He was a big man with a bald head, scald-pink skin, and lines of wrinkles in his neck, like a sharpei or one of those pug dogs with the curly tails that meant you had to look at their butts when they walked away. His mouth opened wide as if he were going to say more, but he stopped. Ran his beady-eyed gaze over Miles. Not unkindly, but still.

Miles shuddered and ducked his head.

The girl he always sparred with stood in the corner of the gym by the foldable bleachers. She had her helmet on, along with a black shirt and a pair of black tights, and she was poking at the blue floor mat with the knobby end of her foil. She was really going at it—the mat had dimpled unattractively as a result of her efforts and sad clumps of gray stuffing were visible.

"I'm pissed at you," she warned as he approached.

"Why?" Miles asked, picking up his own foil and sliding on his mask.

"You left me alone last week. I had to spar with that asshole." The girl cocked her head toward the other side of the room, but Miles didn't know what asshole she might be referring to. It could be anybody.

"I was sick," he told her.

"Oh, yeah? That's convenient. Maybe give me some warning next time, okay? I can be sick, too, you know. I can be anything. I can even forge a damn note from the doctor. How 'bout that?"

"I had a seizure."

The girl stopped jabbing at the mat. She didn't look up or anything, and it was hard to tell through the mesh of her helmet and his, but to Miles it felt like she was staring at him. Glaring, really, and she did it for a while, the glaring, before finally lifting her foil up and pointing it at him. "Whatever," she said. "I don't need to know about how fucked up your brain is. Keep it to yourself."

Miles nodded, but felt his cheeks burn beneath his mask.

He took a deep breath.

Then he lifted his own foil to meet hers.

After spending forty-five minutes instructing high school students on various ways to kill one another, the fencing teacher raised the white flag. Actually, what he did was toss his coffee cup in the trash, grumble something like, "should've stayed in my goddamn bed this morning," and waved them all on their way, but it was definitely a form of surrender. Miles understood that.

This left ten minutes to change and get ready for second-period classes. For Miles that would be social studies, which didn't involve dueling but still felt draining. He put his fencing gear away, along with everyone else, then slipped into the boys' room. But rather than head to the showers or sinks to wash up, he sat down on the metal bench that ran between the lockers.

And waited.

For *something.*

But nothing happened. His own surrender hung limply and unseen. After checking and double-checking that no one was in his immediate vicinity, Miles slid his gym shorts off. Socks, too. The cold air quickened his pulse. He wriggled as fast as he could back into a pair of faded jeans, but his sense of failure failed to dissipate. If anything, it grew sharper, bolder, because one room over, separated by mere plastic sheeting and institutional tile, all the other guys from fencing class were doing things Miles longed desperately not to know about: They snapped towels at each other's asses and turned the hot water on high. They filled the air with moisture and crassness and shouted about tits they'd seen and the size of their dicks and whether or not their girlfriends liked to squeeze the zits on their backs.

Eventually the other guys turned off the hot water. They spilled from the showers to the rows of lockers, tracking their wet footprints all over the place, still talking, still joking. A few insults—"fucking loser" and "look at that asshole"—were thrown in his direction, but that was all. They got dressed. Applied body spray. Grabbed their belongings.

Then they were gone.

Miles's muscles melted then, like soft butter on a hot pan, with all the pain implied in that, and he slumped over onto the bench with one shoulder. He lay there, very still, as his heart whooshed and his hair clung to his skin, damp with sweat and steam.

Being alone was better than not, he reminded himself. Then again, seeing as he was always alone, no matter where he went or who he was with, maybe the sad truth was he just didn't know any better.

# *chapter seventeen*

*What do you like to do for fun?*

Emerson stared at the paper in front of him, fingers clenched around a nubby and tooth-worn no. 2 pencil. This question was inane. Pointless, really. More pointless than most school assignments, since it was a question being posed by a group of students who had designed this survey as part of their latest research methods project. Whatever Emerson wrote down was just throwaway data for them to use—an exercise for someone else and not worth putting any effort into. And seriously, what the hell was *fun* anyway? It was one of those words that belonged with concepts like *happiness* and *joy*, ideas that seemed nice enough until you realized they didn't mean anything. Emerson knew for a fact that you couldn't measure fun or bottle up bliss. Things like that were just abstractions, names for what you called the moments between sorrow.

The multiple-choice options read:

a) spend time with friends or family
b) play sports or be active
c) watch television, play video games, spend time online
d) art or craft type of hobby
e) other—please describe________________________

Emerson couldn't resist rolling his eyes. And he couldn't resist pressing graphite to paper, circling the letter (e), and readying himself to scrawl "jacking off" in the space provided.

Then he stopped.

The hairs on the back of his neck rose up. Emerson turned to his left, sneaking a glance over his shoulder while trying to look like he was doing anything but. May sat two rows back, wearing a hunter green miniskirt, and she crossed and uncrossed her legs while he watched. From what he could tell, she was either daydreaming hard or thinking deeply about whatever the hell it was she did for fun. Her head was lowered and her reading glasses were on, but instead of writing anything down, she twirled her ballpoint pen around and around the tops of her fingers. It was a balancing trick Emerson had never mastered; the blue pen whipped and spun across her knuckles like magic.

His mouth went dry. She couldn't know what had happened between them at that party, up in that bathroom. There was no way.

He'd *feel* it if she did.

Wouldn't he?

Swallowing hard, Emerson peeked next to his right. Sadie Su sat one row behind him and two seats over, beside a wide bay window where autumn sun flooded in and lit her dark hair so that it glowed like fire. He stared openly at her. He couldn't help himself.

Just then, Sadie looked up.

Caught his eye.

And smiled.

Emerson bolted like a racehorse once class was over, long legs carrying him down a flight of stairs and past the school auditorium toward the door that led to the courtyard outside, but it was May who caught up with him. Not Sadie.

He wasn't sure which was worse.

"Hey," she said, reaching for his arm. "Wait up."

"Oh, hey." Emerson slowed his stride. He tried to sound casual. Like he wasn't trying to outrun her. Like he wasn't so jumpy he was on the verge of losing his goddamn mind right there in the middle of C Building, while waves of other students pushed past them, using elbows and backpacks like machetes in order to clear the way. A flash of darkness stirred inside Emerson. One that made him want to shove back. Kick a foot out and trip somebody. Laugh when they fell.

But he didn't do any of that. Instead, he took a deep breath. Pushed his hair back as he looked down at May.

She was biting her bottom lip, and what he saw pooling in her pretty brown eyes shoved at Emerson harder than any jabbing elbow or asshole kid racing against the bell. Because what he saw there was insecurity.

Shame.

Doubt.

Not about him, but about *herself.*

*Shit.*

"I tried calling you all weekend," she said.

"Yeah, sorry about that." Emerson pressed a sheepish grin onto his face. "I was with my family. My brother came home from the hospital on Saturday. It was all kinds of hectic. You know how it is."

"How is he?"

"Miles? He's good. Pretty good."

She nodded, but there were streaks of red coating her throat, staining the top of her chest—crimson-on-brown, like a rueful songbird in spring. "Look, I just wanted to apologize. About Friday. Getting drunk like that was stupid. Really stupid. Humiliating, actually. I mean, I can't remember *anything*."

"Don't apologize," he said.

"But—"

"Please."

She nodded again, less tentative this time, but the red streaks remained. "Let me say thank you, then. Leigh told me you took care of me. That you got me home safe. I don't know how to repay you."

"You don't have to do anything. It was nothing, M."

"It was definitely something."

Emerson shrugged, wishing like hell she'd change the subject or let him go so he could hang himself or cut his wrists or jump off a goddamn roof, but that's when she leaned forward, rose up on the tips of her toes, and kissed him on the lips. Quickly, but not too quickly. Emerson was stunned, totally taken aback, but she tasted good, so good, and her touch was everything he'd dreamed of, warm, powerful, a tumbling force of nature he couldn't deny.

So he let himself do what he'd wanted to do for so long. In front of the whole school, he held her closer. He kissed her deeper. Because he had to erase the self-doubt and shame pooling in her eyes.

He had to.

It *killed* him to see it.

# *chapter eighteen*

Sadie thought, if anything, Dr. Call-Me-Tom looked *more* disheveled this week than last. Maybe this was because they were meeting in a different office, one that made her wonder who he must've pissed off in order to justify the move. The new space was smaller, was situated uncomfortably close to the administrative bathrooms, and came with a scarred metal desk that looked like it had survived the days of mass polio vaccinations and mandatory lice checks.

He'd brought his dumpy laptop with him, along with his rolling chair, although he clearly hadn't had time to unpack. A few milk crates and recycled banker's boxes were shoved haphazardly into a corner, and the only thing on the wall was a bright-colored poster distastefully labeled a "Feelings Chart." The Feelings Chart consisted of a repeated line-drawn character whose frowned and pouted and pulled faces meant to show off his/her emotional state. Sadie wasn't sure if the chart was intended to teach her how to express herself or how to understand others, but seeing as both endeavors were pretty much scraping the bottom of her priority barrel she asked Dr. CMT if he could move it to the opposite wall.

"Why?" he asked.

"So I don't have to look at it."

"The poster bothers you to look at?"

"It's unattractive. It bothers me to look at things that are unattractive. Especially when there are eyes involved."

"Eyes," he echoed.

Sadie waved a hand. "I don't like looking at all those eyes. There's a lot of them on there in case you hadn't noticed."

"You're saying you don't want to be watched."

"Do *you* want to be watched?"

"The poster doesn't bother me."

"Well, you're not the one looking at it, are you?"

He paused. "Why don't we explore your experiences with being watched, Sadie. Could you say more about that?"

"No."

"Excuse me?"

"I said no. Aren't you supposed to be good at this listening thing? Isn't that what therapy is? I tell you things and you listen, and then I go home and have sex dreams about you or whatever?"

He gaped. "Is *that* what you think therapy is?"

"Ask me about my experiences with watching," Sadie instructed. "That's more interesting than being watched. Because sometimes I see things I shouldn't."

For a moment, Dr. CMT didn't answer. He pulled at his unattractively pink ear. He stared at his computer screen. Sadie understood he was torn between discomfort and his desire to challenge her, but he had to know there was nothing to be gained from trying to get the upper hand with her. That was the thing with psychologists, counselors, helping professionals, whatever boring category they wanted to identify with these days. Deep down they were all people pleasers. It's why they did what they did. They cared about being liked, and they cared what other people thought about them. Sadie, on the other hand, cared about nothing. So she could do this challenge thing all day, every day, and never break a damn sweat.

Not once.

"Tell me about your experiences with watching," Dr. CMT finally said with a sigh. "What have you seen that you shouldn't?"

Sadie pushed a smile onto her face, waving that smug flag of victory. "Oh, all sorts of things. For starters, I see the way my mom looks at men before she fucks them."

"Wait, I'm sorry. Your mother is single?"

"No. She's married to my dad."

He blinked. "What religion are your parents, Sadie?"

"My father's an atheist. My mother's Catholic."

"What about you?"

"Me? I'm pathological."

Dr. CMT didn't smirk or respond. He typed something into his computer. "So does your father see what you see? The way your mother looks at men?"

"No. He doesn't see anything. Because he's not here."

"Where is he?"

Sadie shrugged. "I haven't seen him since February."

"You haven't seen your father since February?"

"Nope."

"I'm afraid I don't understand."

"There's nothing to understand. And it's certainly nothing to be afraid of. He's a filmmaker. He does a lot of work with human rights groups. Last I heard he was going to Sudan to film a documentary about education reform or something, but I don't think he's there anymore."

"So where is he?"

"I don't know. He hasn't told us."

"I see." Wrinkles appeared in Dr. CMT's brow, and judging by the Feelings Chart, this meant he was worried. Or confused.

Sadie used her nails to pick at the pills on the shag couch cushions where she sat, collecting them neatly in her cupped hand. "It's not that big a deal. And my mom can do what she wants. I mean, I would if I were her. But that's not the only thing I saw this week."

"It's not?"

"Mmmm, no. See, I went to this party Friday night, and I saw something there. I kind of want to talk to you about it."

"Okay. What sort of party was this?"

Sadie shrugged. "Typical high school shit. Drinking games. Heavy petting. Music that makes you want to blow your brains out—"

"Blow your brains out?"

"It's a metaphor. Jesus."

"Fine. Go on."

"Can I ask you a question, Tom?"

"You can ask me anything. Whether or not I answer is a different story."

Sadie bristled at this, and when she was sure he was looking, she dumped the handful of shag pills straight onto the floor. "I want to know what it's called when a guy is with a girl, and that girl is passed out drunk, like, completely trashed, you know? And let's say this guy, he's taking care of this girl because she's puked all over herself or something, I don't know exactly. So then he takes her clothes off, not to *do* anything to her. Not at first. He does it to help her clean up, I guess. But while he's doing this, he gets sort of turned on, and he—"

"She can't consent to sex while she's intoxicated," Dr. CMT said firmly. "No one can. What you're describing is rape, Sadie. This is something you saw? Or is this something that happened to you?"

"No, this didn't happen to *me*. That's just it, though. What if the guy *doesn't* rape her? He doesn't even touch her. What he does do, though, is, you know." Sadie leaned back and made the gesture with her hands.

The therapist's eyes widened with comprehension, and now the Feelings Chart told her the look on his face was *disgust*.

"He did that . . . in front of her?" he asked. "Really?"

"Worse," Sadie said, with a pinch of pleasure and a whole hell of a lot of satisfaction. "*On* her."

# *chapter nineteen*

The words started up again the moment Miles stepped off campus at the end of the school day.

"Hey, bitch," someone called out from behind him. "Wait up."

Miles didn't respond or look back. He didn't have to. This was the same cat-and-mouse game he'd been acting out his entire life, and while the stripes on the cat might change, or the cat might even be related to him, he was still always, always the mouse.

Even when he was the bitch.

"Why you walking so fast?"

"Slow down, sweetheart."

Pain burrowed in his chest. A part of him wanted to give up right then, just lie down and await whatever brutality was undoubtedly in store. That wasn't a death wish, either, but a strategic analysis of the situation and a desire to conserve resources. Miles understood full well that if asked why he was walking so fast, it meant he was already trapped.

Still, his mind cycled reliably through the options, hopeless as they all were. He could try and run to get away from the guys who were trailing him. Or he could stop and do something submissive and hope they'd get bored. There was a third option, too, of course, which involved Miles doing nothing but what he was already doing—walking the deserted Sonoma streets in his slouchy way and not responding.

Inevitably, this was the inaction he always chose.

Inevitably, it never made a difference.

To others, he was worth the sacrifice. Nothing more.

So Miles kept walking. His mind hummed and rattled. Something about *this* day felt different, though. There was a twist in the wind. A certain slant to the sky. He pushed his feet forward and felt the sidewalk beneath him turn sticky and malleable. It was almost as if he'd fallen straight into a Dali painting or some separate corner of the universe where the laws of nature could be broken. Where past suffering didn't predict future pain.

Or maybe that was just wishful thinking.

He rounded the next corner, turning down a new street and leaving behind the long row of stucco homes with their sagging porches and unwatered lawns. He'd hoped to find human life here—a convenience store, a park full of mothers and their children—enough that continuing to follow him wouldn't outweigh the risk. But in his harried state, he'd miscalculated. This road he'd turned onto wasn't one Miles had seen before, which was strange, considering he'd grown up here. Rather than safety or familiarity, however, everything before him was desolate and bleak, a wide stretch of dimpled asphalt lined with nothing but the vast expanse of a deserted walnut orchard.

Miles didn't falter or turn back. He stayed the course, which was his game plan, after all. Besides, it was always possible the guys weren't going to actually *do* anything to him.

*Oh, anything's possible, boy,* the wind whispered, raspy words running up his spine like a secret. To his right, a group of pigeons pecked and scratched in the yellow grass. Miles shivered. The orchard was long dead and the walnut trees stood in the sun like an army of corpses, their prickled limbs twisting toward the sky like a call for help. Other than the talking wind, the only sound in the air was the whine-hum zapping off the electrical wires strung down the opposite side of the street, and the hurried rush of footsteps coming up behind him.

The first blow landed on the left side of his head. The second, in the small of his back. Miles cried out as he fell forward, legs crumpling beneath him. The foreground flipped as he landed, face hitting the dirt, and the pigeons flapped their wings, fluttering away in a downward rush.

Pain exploded. His world grew louder.

The hum became a *roar*.

# *chapter twenty*

"Mmmm," May murmured as she squirmed and writhed beneath Emerson, her breath hot on his neck. "Don't stop, Em. Please."

They were in her second-floor bedroom on top of her four-poster bed, with their clothes half off, their bodies pressed together, soft sheets twisted around their ankles. May's parents both worked and her little sister was at cheer practice, which meant this moment was theirs alone. Emerson took May's lead and kept doing the thing she didn't want him to stop doing. He did it faster, then slower, then in little circles like he'd read about online. It seemed to work. She arched her back. She shivered and gasped, pushing her face against his chest, her fingers into his skin, and when it was over and she fell against him, Emerson wondered if it had always been this easy. If all this time, all he'd needed to have her was for her to feel self-doubting.

If only he'd known.

May pushed his hand away and rolled on to her side. She whispered in his ear, telling him how good he'd made her feel and filling Emerson with a heady sense of pride and lust. Both sins, he reminded himself, deadly ones, and when she reached down toward his boxers and tried to return the favor, he stopped her.

"What's wrong?" she asked.

He shook his head. He felt weird all of a sudden. He couldn't explain it.

"Em?"

A faint chiming came from across the room, the back pocket of his discarded jeans. Emerson sat up, welcome for the distraction, the opportunity to lie.

"My phone," he said, crawling from the bed. "I'm sorry. I have to answer it."

"Where are you?" his mother snapped when he picked up, making his heart leap. She was using her emergency voice: all clipped and business-like.

"With a, uh, friend. What's wrong?"

"It's your brother. You need to get home."

"Shit." Emerson pushed his hair back. May turned and stared at him. "Another seizure?"

"No." She told him how a truck driver had found Miles collapsed on the side of the road out near Jack London Way. The cops brought him home after getting him checked out at urgent care. It looked like he'd been beaten up. Bloody nose. Bruised ribs. Possible concussion.

"I need you," his mother said again, her business voice slipping. "The cops, they're still here."

"I'm coming," Emerson told her, and he hung up.

He looked back at May, sprawled on the bed in the dying afternoon light with her hair down and her dark breasts still bared. The lesser part of him wanted to touch her again, feel her all over, breathe her in. It was a crazy sort of urge, given the phone call he'd just received and the thing that had happened between them over the weekend. But maybe urges like this were nature's reminders that they were mere animals. That all humans were driven by hormones and pheromones and biological imperatives, only to be copiloted by a mind that could rationalize it all. Then again, what he'd done Friday night, Emerson couldn't rationalize. But he felt guilty about it. That had to count for something. Guilt meant he wasn't like Sadie Su, who did things, not in spite of their badness. She did them *because* they were bad.

That was something different altogether.

Emerson's lust withered into crawling dread. Of all the people in the world, *Sadie* had to be the one to walk in. He'd never be able to talk sense into her, explain that what she saw didn't matter, so long as May never found out. He just had to hope against hope that she'd keep her dumb mouth shut. She would, if she knew what was good for her. Then again, it was Sadie.

Sadie, who never listened to reason.

Sadie, who believed cruelty was a virtue.

Sadie, who was the exception always, always willing to prove the rule.

The sky was darkening by the time he reached the apartment complex, and Emerson squeezed the Mustang into the carport with mere inches to spare. The asshole next door with the Suburban had parked over the white line again, and Emerson was lucky not to rip his side mirror clean off.

He cut the ignition, took the key out, and sat there. The old car settled with its usual pings and sighs and shuddering under-the-hood rattles, and with his own internal organs doing pretty much the same thing, Emerson realized he didn't want to go in and face whatever hell was going on with his brother. He just didn't. He knew it was terrible of him to feel that way. Miles was a victim. Someone had *hurt* him. That should make Emerson want to wring the necks of whoever had jumped his little brother.

And yet . . .

And yet, Emerson couldn't finish that thought. It was too horrible. Too heartless. He was better than that, or at least he *wanted* to be. What he could do, however, was slide out the bottle of whisky he'd hidden under the front seat last week—Johnnie Walker, Red Label, nabbed from the corner store in a dark moment of impulse and opportunity—and hold it between his legs. The shape of it, the weight, the slosh of the brown liquid all comforted him. The funny thing was, he'd stored the emergency booze in the Mustang *prior* to Trish Reed's party. Before he even knew he'd need it. Like he was psychic or something.

Actually, Emerson realized, that wasn't very funny at all.

The wind whipped through the trees outside, wild and rattling, and after a glance in the rearview mirror, Emerson unscrewed the bottle top and took a furtive swallow. Then another. He didn't go crazy or anything. Just downed enough to feel a little warm and like he wasn't about to jump out of his damn skin.

After a few minutes, he drank more.

Maybe too much.

Emerson finally got out of the car and walked upstairs.

When he opened the front door to the apartment, the first thing he saw was a cop, a female one. She sat in the living room with her legs crossed like it was fucking high tea, talking to his mom. Another cop, this one a man, stood in the kitchen jabbering away on his phone.

At the sight of him, his mother rushed over, bringing with her a whole flurry of emotion, all tears and need. Emerson understood: the last time the cops had been here, it'd been to arrest her. He and Miles had gone to social services for three horrible weeks. Clearly his mother remembered this, too, because she wrapped her arms around Emerson and didn't let go. Dipping his knees and hugging her back, he winced at the thinness of her bones, the new streaks of gray in her hair. He prayed she couldn't smell the alcohol on his breath.

He prayed he would never disappoint her.

"This your other son?" The lady cop turned to look at him. She was different than most of the police officers Emerson had interacted with over the years, the ones with the beer guts and alimony payments who hung around the basketball games and vacillated between wanting to kiss his ass or beat some respect into him. This one looked like she didn't care about sports or rivalries or small-town pride. She was young, with steely eyes and sharp features like a fox or a weasel.

His mother stepped back and patted his arm proudly. "This is my Emerson. My eldest."

"Where's Miles?" he asked her.

"Resting."

"Is he okay?"

Her eyes puddled. "I should check on him."

By the hurried way she left the room, it was clear she wouldn't be back. This was her escape.

"I'm Detective Gutierrez," the lady cop called out.

Emerson walked over. Shook her hand. He felt jumpy, filled with the breakaway need to talk, and in a way, despite his guilt and paranoia, Emerson was grateful for the Johnnie Walker. It glossed his edges. Slowed him down.

"What happened to my brother?" he asked the cop.

"That's what we're trying to figure out."

"How bad is he hurt?"

"He'll be okay. He's mostly shaken up. Some bruises. The burns. It's more . . ."

*Burns?* "More what?"

"He won't tell us what happened."

"Maybe he doesn't know."

She frowned. "He's making it hard for us to help him."

Sounds like Miles, Emerson wanted to say, but didn't. His glossed edges were quickly turning fuzzy.

"Can I ask you some questions, Emerson?" Detective Gutierrez asked.

*About my brother?*

*Or about me?*

"Sure," he said evenly. "Why not?"

This book is insane

## *chapter twenty-one*

Roman was writing on an almost daily basis now.

It was driving Sadie a little batty.

Day or night, his rambling, heartfelt messages traveled to her via airwave or satellite signal or the goddamn space-time continuum, and she was helpless to do anything about it. Sadie read his messages, though. Every single one. They seemed like a good thing to monitor, in case he started making bomb threats or referring to himself as the Minister of Death.

Only nothing that interesting had happened, unfortunately. Roman was still the same boring old Roman, and she could just picture him hunched in front of his computer, tapping out his loneliness, keystroke by dour keystroke. His overall tone had changed, though: there were no more shy pleas or bashful questions. Instead, it seemed, he was putting it all out there—converting his thoughts and existential despair into words and sending them to her, completely unedited. Sadie never responded, of course, so she really didn't understand what the point was.

Unless, of course, that *was* the point.

Tonight, however, it was after midnight, and she still hadn't heard from him. She had gotten a few texts from Wilderness Camp Chad, but those she deleted unread. When she needed him, he'd be there. That was all that mattered.

Instead of sleeping, Sadie sat cross-legged on her bed with a notebook in her lap and a fancy pen she'd stolen from her therapist's office. It was the only nice thing he had in there, and she decided it might as well be hers. After all, he was the one who'd given her this crappy therapy homework to do in the first place.

Per his instructions, she was meant to be writing down Responsible Actions She Could Take in light of what she'd caught Emerson doing at that dumb party, along with the possible consequences of those actions. Dr. CMT had said the exercise would be a way for her to understand the weight of her own decisions. He'd also used words like "sexual assault" and "serious violation" and "ethical responsibility."

So she wrote:

*I could . . .*

- Tell the girl.
- Tell the police.
- Tell everyone.

Sadie sat back. She looked at her words and admired the backward slant of her handwriting. The thing was, the consequences of all these actions were the same: Emerson would get in trouble. Maybe even go to jail or at least get suspended and put on some kind of pervert watch list. People would see him for the creep he was, and maybe he'd stop staring at her in class in that dippy way he'd been doing, like a dim-witted dog whose bone had been stolen right out from under its nose.

Of course, it was equally possible she could tell and he *wouldn't* get in trouble. You heard about that happening on the news all the time. Guys did things to girls, worse than Emerson, and nobody cared. Sadie supposed she should feel some sort of outrage over that or a sense of righteousness, but she didn't. Being outraged about anything was a waste of time. You didn't gain anything by being mad or even by being right. Besides, most people would be outraged with her if they knew half the things she'd done in her lifetime.

Ultimately, it came down to a matter of leverage: if Sadie told, then Emerson's secret wouldn't be *hers*. It'd be useless. She'd have no power over him, and there was no damn fun in that.

So she wrote down a few other ideas:

*I could . . .*

- Make friends with the girl.
- Blackmail Emerson.
- Drive him insane.
- Get him to do anything.

"Screw responsibility," she whispered, and right then her phone buzzed. Sadie looked down. It was an email. From Roman. Setting pen and notebook aside, she pushed back her scalloped-edge sheets and swung her feet to the floor. For some reason, she couldn't read his words to her here, in her own room. There was only one place in the house she felt comfortable doing that, and it's where she was headed.

But first, the bathroom; Sadie needed to pee. She let her toes tap on cold tile while she sat on the toilet. When she was done, she hopped up and pulled her nightgown down. She didn't bother wiping. Sadie liked the warmth on her thighs almost as much as she liked breaking rules.

Creeping downstairs on soft feet, she found the whole house midnight dark and midnight still. There was no sign of her mom anywhere, thank God, or any of her mom's friends. That was the word her mom used to describe the people she was screwing around with behind Sadie's dad's back. Regular people and family were introduced by name, but the quick fucks and boozy gropers and pool boys with tight abs and good weed, well, those were *friends.* Hell, for all Sadie knew, the term wasn't a euphemism, and her mother actually believed banging someone and never calling them back was the true definition of friendship.

Hell, for all Sadie knew, maybe it was.

Making her way down darkened hallways and through shadowy rooms, she arrived at a closed door on the north end of the house. Sadie pushed her way in. The cool scent of rotting books filled her nostrils. All the lamps were dust-coated and in disuse, but moonlight washed through the tall windows, guiding her toward her destination—a leather armchair that was situated in the tight spot between a long-cold hearth and her father's prized gun collection. Never a hunter, he admired the craftsmanship. And power. Sadie did, too. Every once in a while, she slipped one of the old pistols from the case, loaded it, and held it in her lap. Just to know what it felt like. But tonight she didn't bother. She flopped down, gathered her legs beneath her, and pulled a camel-colored cashmere throw around her shoulders to preserve heat.

She held her phone up.

She opened Roman's message.

She read his words to her.

Hey, Sadie.

It's late, I know. Late here, anyway, and it's just . . . I've got a lot on my mind. Sometimes that means I'm up all night long, and other days I can't get myself out of bed. I don't know. That's odd, I guess. Like if even my depression can't be consistent, what hope is there for the rest of me?

I'm also not sure how to feel about this homeschooling thing. Truthfully, I feel like an oversheltered child, even though my mom's not the one teaching me. I'm teaching myself most of the time or watching videos online, so it's not like autonomy is an issue. But it's still weird. At Rothshire the school was our home, right? That was homeschooling in a way. So why do I feel like this? Maybe I've just been gone so long this place doesn't feel like home anymore. There are still leaves on the trees here in Kentucky. People in shorts, girls wearing tank tops or hanging out in those flimsy sun dresses and plastic sandals. They soak up warmth when all I want is to be cold. That's funny, too, isn't it? To want so badly what it was that almost killed me.

I wish I could explain what it was like, that night in the snow, beneath the brightest stars and the fullest moon. I was surrounded by ice, no matter where I went, no matter what I did. It was terrible and it was beautiful, and I don't remember everything—just the blood and the pain—but when I try and talk about that night, no one wants to listen. They either change the subject or ask if I'm feeling better, and it's like I'm doing the wrong thing by not wanting to hold it all inside. Should I be embarrassed? I'm not. I'm not anything, these days, if you want to know the truth. Maybe that's what's wrong with me.

Maybe that's why you did what you did.

It's one of my theories anyway. That you wanted me to die because my life isn't worth living. That you were punishing me for my weaknesses. I have a lot of theories, though, and I think I want to tell them to you. I also think you have to listen. Because unlike a science lab or a math proof or a miracle from God, there's nothing in the outside world that can tell me if I've stumbled onto the truth. Only something that lives inside of you can do that.

And only you know what that something is.

—R

# *chapter twenty-two*

*What were the origins of pain?*

Miles's mind fluttered into wakefulness. He lay very still. He took stock of where he was. He was in his own room, pressed beneath the cool sheets of his bed. Moonlight drifted through the air, a lost traveler on a dark night, and Miles could see that Emerson's bed was empty. He was probably on the couch beneath a pile of old blankets. That was where his brother always slept when he was ill or hurting. Or when he couldn't stand Miles for reasons that were never, ever spoken out loud.

Miles tried pushing himself to sitting. He groaned and fell back. Clutched at his side.

Every part of him hurt.

*So much.*

He tried again. This time, he took a deep breath, braced for the pain and forced his body up, all the way, moving against the ache in his ribs and the sting of his muscles. Once on his feet, he shuffled across the room on stiff legs to the far window. There he leaned against the metal frame and stared out at the night.

Midnight silence. Nothing of interest was out there—neglected trees, old cars, small pieces of trash rolling around in the breeze—but still, something both ancient and new stirred within him. Like the sweep and turn of a compass dial, Miles felt himself teetering on the edge of some temporal horizon, that narrowing border between now and yet-to-come.

There was still a twist to the wind. There was still a slant to the sky.

Like the origin of his pain, his truth was so close.

It scratched and growled,
it slumbered and snored,
just a room away,
all while the wind knocked
and whispered
*get ready for your shine, boy*
*get your soul good and ready*
*the end is coming*
*the truth'll be here*
*soon.*

# *chapter twenty-three*

Morning came in its inevitable way. A bright and bitter end.

Dots of gray mist and pink haze crept over the eastern hills, lighting the room and stirring Sadie from sleep. She yawned and stretched, then crawled from her father's armchair back upstairs for a shower. After she was scrubbed clean, Sadie stared at herself in the full-length mirror in her room for a few minutes, wet hair dripping all over the place. It was something she did a lot, eyeing her naked form from all different angles, wondering if she'd ever see anything different. Echoes of her father, perhaps: a hint of his warmth, his compassion.

Sadie didn't see any of that.

She never did.

Turning away from the mirror, she yawned again and rubbed her eyes. Her rest had been fitful—dreams about Roman *needing* things from her, God—and after putting on clothes and blow-drying her hair, Sadie craved coffee something bad. Making chit-chat with her mom in the kitchen while they pot-watched the French press felt unbearable, so she moved deftly to Plan B. This involved grabbing her school stuff, lifting a twenty from the pile of cash that had been set out to pay the house cleaner, and slipping from the house to her car before the sun could dry the dew-damp grass.

She cranked the stereo and nosed the Jetta down the drive. A flock of wild turkeys huddled along the dirt shoulder, looking like the world's ugliest clusterfuck. As she passed them, the birds gobbled and cooed and appeared to be in a state of great excitement. It took Sadie a moment to realize they were all watching a big tom strut his stuff right in the middle of the main road. His red throat thing was flapping in the wind, his tail feathers were spread wide, and did turkeys have balls? If they did, his were probably swinging like mad.

Sadie didn't bother honking. She just gunned the car forward.

In town, the main square had a Starbucks. Two, in fact, including one with a drive-through, but Sadie hated Starbucks with a passion usually reserved for people who lied to her, bored her, or did something gross like picked earwax in public or chewed ice with their mouths open. So she headed out to a strip mall near the highway.

The coffee shop next to the Motel 6 was decent enough, but the lot was crowded this early in the morning. Filled with wine reps and wine regret, no doubt. Sadie was forced to park outside the 7-11, which was how she ended up noticing the strange boy from her fencing class, who was crouched behind the Dumpster, puking into a plastic bag.

Again.

Sadie waited until she had an unlit cigarette and double vanilla latte in hand before marching over to gawk at him.

"Ew," she said.

The boy twitched and looked up. His eyes were watery and pink, and despite the white Safeway bag he held tight in his hands, there were obvious flecks of barf on his crappy knock-off sneakers. Hole in the bag, apparently.

Sadie thought about cracking a joke or teasing him or telling him straight out how damn pathetic and vile this whole thing was, but she noticed other things, too: a bandaged forearm, deep bruising on one cheek, the awkward way he held his ribs. Plus, there was something in the way the boy stared back at her—wide-eyed and sad and so very, very lost—that for the first time, in a long while, Sadie restrained herself.

"You look like shit," she told him. "Utter shit."

He nodded quickly, but his muscles bunched. Like he was going to make a run for it.

"Come on," she said. "Don't do that. Look, I'll give you a ride, okay?"

"Don't puke in my car," she instructed when the boy had gotten settled in the Jetta's front seat and they were back on the road.

"I won't," he said firmly.

True to his word, the boy rode like a well-trained dog, with his thin shoulders tensed and his nostrils flared and his shaggy blond hair flopping in his eyes and snaking down toward his collar. Sadie watched him out of the corner of her eye. God, he looked so *young*. Not that she was some advanced age, but he had the mannerisms of a child. Of something slight and fearful.

"How old are you, anyway?" she asked.

"Fifteen."

"Jesus. No one's going to put out an Amber Alert or anything if I'm driving around with you, are they?"

"Huh?"

"How'd you get that bruise on your face?"

"I don't want to talk about it."

"Fine. Tell me what foods you're allergic to, then. Why are you always getting sick?"

It took the boy a moment to answer, and when he did, his words came slowly, as if he needed to handle them with great care. "I have sensitivities to gluten. Lactose. Soy, maybe. And onions. My allergist is still running tests."

Sadie laughed out loud. She couldn't help it. She clasped her hand over her mouth, but it wasn't like the boy didn't notice. She was, after all, laughing at him.

"Is that funny?" he asked.

"Come on. Onions are pretty fucking funny. I mean, they're *onions.* No one has to eat onions. Most people don't even like them. It's not like you're a diabetic who's allergic to insulin or something." She pulled another cigarette out and stuck it in her mouth while the lighter warmed. "Tell me what you had for breakfast."

"Cereal."

She glanced over at him. "Gluten free?"

"Fruit Loops."

"Oh, *damn,* kid. Living dangerously, huh? With cow's milk, too, I bet. Is that right?"

"Yeah."

The lighter popped out then, all glowing and red, and this time, when Sadie laughed, she thought she saw the boy's lips twist into the very faintest of smiles.

# *chapter twenty-four*

Guilt utilized its own kind of magic.

This was Emerson's realization when he woke up Tuesday morning on the living-room couch to find his stomach sour with post-whisky resentment, and both Miles and his mother already gone. Guilt didn't manifest itself in the expected ways. It was trickier than that, capable of all sorts of transpositions and sleights of hand.

He groaned and pulled himself up to sitting. Sleep hadn't come easy for him last night. After the cops left, it took two more trips to the Mustang and the Johnnie Walker bottle before he was able to lie down and rest. Even then, when he finally shut his eyes, he hadn't dreamed of May or Sadie or even his strange little brother who was apparently so danger prone he needed a guardian angel or one of those hermetically sealed plastic bubbles to help keep him alive.

No, Emerson had dreamed about the cat. The tabby one with the blue suede collar with the bell on it. He'd dreamed about that damn creature all night long, as if some phantom recording device inside his head were rewinding and replaying the memory of him hitting it, over and over, until it was etched into his soul. Until it was distorted into something far more meaningful than it should've been.

In some of the dreams, Emerson didn't actually hit the cat. He was driving down the country lane with Trey and Giovanna in the car, but instead of staring at the crows, he saw the animal dozing in a patch of lazy sun, even before Trey yelled. In those dreams, he was able to honk and swerve at the last minute. The cat would scramble across the road, its wide belly dragging on the ground before vanishing into the bushes with a hot flash of its striped tail.

But in most of the dreams, the cat still died, and what haunted Emerson wasn't seeing its broken neck or glassy eyes or the dot of blood dripping from its nose. It was the sensation of holding its dead body in his hands. The slack weight. The riffling of soft fur in the breeze.

The rush and the reverence that came with witnessing a life slip away into the ether for good.

"I heard about Miles," Trey said when they met up in the hall before third period. "Fuck, man."

"Yeah." Emerson threw his books into his locker. His jacket, too. It was early still, but already everything in the building felt hot and stuffy. Like he was choking. Like he could barely breathe.

"Where is he?"

"I don't know. He's here. Somewhere. We don't ride together."

"You should."

"I guess. He's big on walking."

"Who did it?"

"I don't know."

"You don't know?"

"He won't say. Not even to the cops. I had to talk to them for a long time last night."

Trey leaned forward, dropped his voice to a whisper. "Giovanna said they *burned* him. With a cigarette or something."

Emerson winced. "Yeah."

"That's *sick.* Like, seriously sadistic. Look, we're going to find out who did it, okay? And then we're going to kick their asses. Because he's a kid. A fucking *kid*."

"I guess." Emerson rubbed at his temple.

"You *guess*?"

"I don't know. I mean, if he won't say anything, maybe he doesn't need us to kick anyone's ass. Maybe that's on him. For once."

*"Bullshit,"* Trey said.

"What?"

"I said bullshit. He's just a scared kid. You know Miles. He's always taking crap like that. What he says or doesn't say doesn't change anything."

"Well, maybe he doesn't even know who did it."

Trey's cheeks went flush. "What's *wrong* with you? It's your brother. It doesn't matter if he knows. What matters is what those fuckheads did, and what we're going to do when we find them."

"Yeah, yeah. Fine." Emerson nodded his agreement wearily. He didn't get where all of Trey's anger was coming from and why it was coming at *him*. It wasn't his fault Miles never fought back. But Trey had a point. You couldn't qualify sympathy for an act of violence based on whether or not you liked the victim. Wrong was wrong.

Right?

"You okay?" Trey asked. "You look weird."

Emerson slammed his locker door shut. "My stomach feels like shit. I couldn't eat this morning."

Giovanna bounced up to them then, smelling like bubble gum and Camel Lights. She hooked her arm through Trey's and kissed his cheek with a smack. She didn't ask about Miles. She didn't ask about anything. Together, the three of them walked to their next class, which was Research Methods. Emerson girded himself inwardly, because May would be in there and he'd have to smile and play at being her boyfriend, which was what he'd wanted, only he hadn't wanted it like this, full of secrets and stress and nightmares about dead cats.

Stepping into the classroom, he glanced over at May's desk. And froze.

Seated right beside her, with her dark hair in braids, was Sadie Su.

Neither girl looked up at Emerson. They were too busy with their heads together, staring down at something on Sadie's phone and laughing.

Emerson took a halting step backward, then another.

"What's he *doing*?" Giovanna said loudly, but Emerson ignored her, along with Trey's questioning stare. He kept walking backward, kept bumping into people.

When he reached the door, he turned and fled.

# *chapter twenty-five*

Miles did his best to move through his Tuesday classes unnoticed, which was always his goal, but somehow the day had become one of people telling him how he should be feeling. Not the girl from fencing who'd given him a ride, thankfully, but pretty much everybody else.

*That must hurt.*

*You must be so pissed.*

*You'd better be scared, bitch. We'll do it again.*

If that weren't bad enough, all the extra attention meant people kept asking him things he would've refused to answer on a good day, much less now.

*How are you doing?*

*Do you want to talk about it?*

*Gonna snitch, fag?*

*Who did it? Who hurt you? Who? Who?*

But the worst thing of all was that people touched him. The whole day long. What was it about being physically violated that invited *more* physical contact? Without even asking? Wherever Miles went, teachers squeezed his shoulders, patted his back. A girl in history class took his hand and rubbed the soft side of his forearm where the bandage and burns were. Horribly, this made tears spring to his eyes, hot and miserable, and when he was called to the principal's office after lunch, the nurse there actually *stroked his bruised cheek,* with the back of her knuckles, like he was a baby. At that point, Miles had to excuse himself to the bathroom to throw up, and he stayed there, drooling and heaving over the sink like a dyspeptic dog until one of the office assistants came and knocked on the door.

"You gotta go home if you're sick," she said when he came out.

"What?"

"If you're vomiting or have diarrhea, you have to stay home from school for twenty-four hours. That's the rule."

It was? Miles thought about this. "Well, then I'd never be at school."

The assistant frowned. "Look, there's a virus going around. We don't want it to spread."

"I don't have a virus."

"Whatever, kid. I don't make these things up."

In the principal's office, Miles told her exactly what he'd told the cops, which was nothing. No, he didn't know who did it. No, he didn't know why. It was the truth, in a way. Because it could've been anybody. And it could only have been him.

It didn't matter. He still ended up in a windowless room, sitting on an ugly couch across from the school's therapist, who was some young guy with wire-rimmed glasses and a nervous habit of rolling his chair around.

Miles did his best to stare intently at the floor, which was probably his own nervous habit—an act he did by pure instinct, like nail biting or hurting himself so that others couldn't hurt him first.

"I'm Dr. MacDougall," the therapist said in this forced cheery voice, like he was trying to sell something not worth the price. "You can call me Tom."

Miles said nothing.

"I'm sorry you were hurt, Miles."

He still said nothing.

"I know it didn't happen on campus, but Principal Abrams thought it would be a good idea for us to talk. About . . . the assault. About your feelings. About anything. Your mother agreed, too."

Miles let his head droop farther, down between his knees. "My mother knows I'm talking to you?"

"Yes."

"Oh."

More silence.

Dr. MacDougall cleared his throat. "Anything you say here is confidential, you know. That means whatever we talk about stays between us. The only time I'd ever have to break confidentiality would be if you told me about any instances of child abuse or elder abuse, or if I felt you were planning to hurt yourself or other people."

"What would you do then?" Miles asked.

"It would depend on what you told me."

"What would you do if you felt I was planning to hurt other people?"

"Are you?"

"I just want to know the answer to the question."

"My priority would be to keep you and everyone else safe."

"How?"

"I would probably have to call the police."

"That's it?"

"If I knew who it was you were planning on hurting, it would be my duty to warn those parties, as well."

Miles nodded. Duty to warn. It's what he'd always believed. That the reason he saw things from the future was so that he could change them. Only, he'd never actually warned anybody about the things he saw. Ever. People kept dying and people kept suffering, even when he knew about it ahead of time.

So maybe his duty was something different.

That's what he was beginning to think, anyway.

"So are you?" Dr. MacDougall asked.

Miles lifted his head for the first time. "Am I what?"

"Are you planning on hurting somebody?"

"Planning's not the same as knowing something's going to happen, is it?"

"No, it's not." The therapist frowned. "But you know, I don't think I'm understanding exactly what it is you're trying to say. Are you saying you know something's going to happen to somebody else?"

Miles wrapped his arms around himself and rubbed his shoulders. Then he leaned forward and pressed the toes of his shoes together, *tap tap tap.* "I'm saying that sometimes the future is our destiny. I'm saying that sometimes we know where we're going, but we're still helpless to stop it. That's what I'm saying. That's what I mean."

# *chapter twenty-six*

Wednesday morning, Sadie stopped by the coffee shop again on her way to school and bought her double vanilla latte. Only Dumpster Boy wasn't there. Not that she was looking for him or anything, but it got her wondering a bit about where he was and what he might be doing, and when she came upon him walking along the side of the road beneath a row of eucalyptus trees, maybe a mile from campus, she felt the tiniest sense of relief. She pulled up behind him and laid on the horn, as hard as she could.

The boy jumped straight into the air. He whirled around to stare at her for a moment. Then he turned and kept walking. He was wearing some ugly T-shirt from a bait shop. It was green and had a cartoon fish with googly eyes on the back.

Sadie eased the car forward, letting the Jetta stay pace with him while she rolled her window down.

"Hey!" she shouted. "Hey, you!"

He didn't respond. Just walked in his weird hunched-shoulder way.

"Hey, asshole. I know you can hear me."

The boy still didn't answer or even acknowledge her presence.

Enough fucking around. Sadie punched the gas and swerved onto the shoulder right in front of him. With the engine still running, she stepped out of the car and stalked back to where he was. "What the hell are you doing? I'm trying to do something nice for you, you know."

Nothing. He said nothing. The boy was too busy staring at the back of her car.

"What are you looking at?" she snapped.

He pointed. "What's that?"

"What?"

"That." He walked forward and placed his hand on the sticker decal on the rear window of the purring car. Soft puffs of exhaust floated toward his legs.

Sadie frowned. "That? Just something dumb. It's from my family's vineyard. Su Vin."

The boy blinked and looked at her with those sad, sleepy eyes of his, like he was seeing her for the first time. "Your family?"

"Yeah. Well, it's our name. Su. My parents don't really have anything to do with the actual winemaking. They used to, when they first bought the property, but not anymore."

"What do they do now?"

"My dad travels. My mom doesn't."

"Why doesn't she?"

"I don't know why."

"Maybe you're the why."

Sadie snorted. "Come on. I'm giving you a ride."

"You don't have to do that."

"Jesus, kid. I know I don't have to. Just get in the damn car, already."

He got in the car and sat down. He tilted his head and gazed at the car's in-dash speaker like he could actually see the music streaming out of it.

"What is this?" he asked.

*"Onegin."*

"What?"

"It's Tchaikovsky."

"What's an Onegin?"

"It's the name of the opera. It was based on a poem by Pushkin. It's about this rich guy named Eugene Onegin who thinks his troubled angsty persona gives him an excuse to be a real dick."

"Ah."

She looked at him. "I heard about what happened to you, you know. How you got hurt the other day."

He shrugged.

"Those guys who did that to you are assholes."

"Whatever."

"Well," she said. "If you're not going to care, I won't, either."

"Thank you."

They rode in silence for a while. But as they approached the school, Sadie peeked over at the boy. "Can I ask you one question, though?"

He nodded. "Okay."

"Two questions actually."

"Sure."

"First. What's your name?"

"Miles," he said.

"I'm Sadie. And Miles, huh? You should be a runner, not a fencer."

"I don't want to be either."

"Fair enough. Second question: Do you think you got jumped by those guys because there's something wrong with you? Or because there's something wrong with them?"

Miles reached to touch the speaker in front of him, his fingers gently traveling across its grooved dips and valleys. "I don't know why people do the things they do. I can only see ahead, into the future. The past doesn't make a lot of sense to me."

"You can see the future?" Sadie asked doubtfully.

He nodded.

"What does it look like?"

"Bad."

"Yeah? No shit. I bet we're all going to die, too."

The boy leaned back in his seat. "There's a lot wrong with me, though. Sometimes I worry that I'm not a very normal person."

Sadie frowned. "What kind of person are you, then?"

"Disturbed." he said, letting his eyes shut with a flutter. "I'm a disturbed person. That's what I am."

In her research class, Sadie sat beside Emerson Tate's girlfriend again. She did it just to be a huge pain in his ass and because she liked the look on his face when he came into the room and saw her, the way he turned all pink and awkward and bumbled his words. The girlfriend, however, clearly liked Emerson, which made Sadie doubt what side of the bell curve her Stanford-Binet quotient fell on. The girl immediately went over to him and started flirting. Poor taste, Sadie thought, even if she didn't know what he'd done to her at that party. Emerson was attractive enough, sure, but he was seriously dull. So very different from when they first knew each other.

"Hey, Emerson," Sadie called out.

"Huh?" He turned and looked at her.

"What's your phone number?"

"Why?"

"I want to send you something. I got a couple pictures of you from the other night."

He blanched.

"So what's your number?" she asked again.

"My phone can't get photo texts," he mumbled.

"What? Why's that?"

"Because I'm poor as shit, Sadie."

The girlfriend piped up. "You can send the pictures to me."

"No. Email me." Emerson came over to Sadie's desk. He picked up her pen and wrote his school address on her notebook. When he was done, he glared at her. She smiled brightly.

Just then, the bell rang and their teacher walked in.

Sadie leaned down and grabbed her bag. She started jamming her stuff away, pen, notebook, navy cardigan sweater. Then she got up from her desk and walked toward the door.

"Where do you think you're going?" the teacher asked.

"Nurse's office," Sadie said over her shoulder. "Cramps."

"That bad?"

She nodded and touched her stomach. "It feels like I'm having a baby."

The teacher ignored the giggling that came from this response. "I want to see a note from the nurse, Miss Su. Or else."

Sadie cruised the halls of the school a little bit, looking for the perfect spot where no one would bug her. There was a new message on her phone from Roman, which was why she'd left. She wanted to read it. Now. But as she strolled farther and farther away from her classroom, Sadie realized she felt good for once. Better than good. Little moments like this were some of the thrills that made life worth living. It was all about perspective, not the facts of the matter. Because the fact of the matter was, walking down the hallway of a grubby overcrowded suburban high school was more than a little unsavory. But walking these halls after screwing with Emerson and weaseling her way out of class with the boldest of lies? Well, that was an act that filled Sadie head to toe with a feeling far better than any of the more corporeal pleasures.

It meant she'd won.

Which was the only thing she cared about.

In a way, it was how she and Roman had met in the first place. Sadie had been caught smoking at Rothshire her first week there. As punishment, she was assigned the job of proctor for the weeknight sophomore study hall and ended up tutoring a football player named Charlie Burns in World History.

"Those flashcards you made Charlie are all wrong," Roman came up and told her one evening, after the rest of the room had cleared out. Sadie had been surprised. He'd never spoken to her before. She had no idea who he was.

"I know they're wrong," she said. "I wrote them. What's it to you?"

"It's nothing to me. I just want to know why you're doing it."

She shrugged. "Maybe there's no why other than the obvious one."

Roman cocked his head. "And what would that be?"

"I mean, it's kind of obvious to me that there would be nothing better on this earth than for Charlie Burns to fill out his World History blue book with statements like 'an oligarchy is a form of government whose ruling class is determined by wishes.' "

Roman had laughed then, a real laugh, deep and rich, and to her surprise, Sadie found that she was laughing, too.

"Maybe I went a little overboard with that one," she admitted.

"No," Roman said. "That's perfect. Charlie Burns, he's not . . . he's not the nicest guy around, if you want to know the truth."

Sadie hadn't responded to this statement. She didn't care one bit about Charlie's niceness. Or anyone's niceness, for that matter. What she objected to was the fact that Charlie Burns was dumber than a nutsack and that he was dating her roommate, thereby ruining Sadie's life by coming to their room all the time and sticking his hand down Lily Monroe's pants. She'd walked in on them on more than one occasion and once they'd actually been going at it *on Sadie's bed.*

But now, as Sadie climbed up the interior stairs of the main classroom building and kicked open a service door to step out onto the gravel and tar-paper roof, she wondered what Roman had meant. About Charlie.

She walked to the roof's edge, sat her butt on the narrow turret, and pulled out a cigarette. Some weird late-season heat wave had snuck into town, and already the sun's strength was unbearable. She stared down at the shade in the courtyard, three long stories away. Then she read his email:

---

Theory #2: your zero-sum mind

George Patton once said "the object of war is not to die for your country but to make the other bastard die for his." I don't know much about war and I don't know that you do either, but this quote reminded me of you. I think you're always at war with everyone and everything. That if you don't win every argument, every point, then you think you've failed. That's why you don't have friends. Friends aren't at war with each other. But we were. Or maybe you were at war with me, and I was just the dying bastard too stupid to realize it.

---

Sadie squared her jaw. She didn't know what to say to that, nor did he appear to be inviting any sort of commentary. So she simply replied:

---

I want to know what happened with you and Charlie Burns.

Tell me.

---

# *chapter twenty-seven*

*A trail of truth for him to follow . . .*

Late in the morning during math class, Miles felt the hum of electricity build inside his body. It was like getting a jolt from an electric fence, only the jolt kept going. And going.

Until his limbs went tingly.

Until his gut went hot.

Until he started to see things in the *right way.*

He knew what was happening, so he raised his hand and asked his algebra teacher if he could go to the bathroom. Or at least, that's what he thought he did. As the tingle and hum of prevision aura washed over him, Miles wasn't sure of very much at all. He could hear his own voice, his inflection stammering and shy, but it sounded like it was coming from the next room, not out of his own mouth. Then, almost as if he were floating, Miles watched as he got up from his desk and walked down the hall like a robot, heading for the room with the mirrors.

*The mirrors.*

In the bathroom, Miles leaned so close to the sink, he got a wet spot on the front of his pants. But for once impending embarrassment didn't make him blush or feel sick to his stomach. He was too busy staring at his own reflection.

He stared.

And stared.

And stared.

Until *click,* like a key in a lock, the future opened, right before him.

It waved him forward. And back.

For one blurred instant, he was standing behind that girl's car again, looking at the sticker in her window.

An *S* and a *V* intertwined.

Su Vin.

Then the car was gone, and Miles was somewhere else, shuttled into the unknown. Somewhere dark and terrible. Here, he saw death again. Along with his own face, pale and miserable.

When Miles next blinked, he was outside, walking in the hot sun with sweat pouring down his back, his thighs. He didn't know where he was or how he'd gotten here or even what time of day it was, but clearly he'd skipped forward in time and stayed there. From the way his shimmery stretch of shadow lay long across the road in this weird October heat and the sky appeared to be darkened, he guessed it was late afternoon.

Far later than it had been.

At least he wasn't being followed again. Miles turned around and around. He was out in the valley somewhere, on the shoulder of the main road where people went wine tasting and apple picking. But how did he get out here?

Why couldn't he remember?

There was a winery up ahead. He put his hand over his brow and squinted. He could make out the white hand-carved road sign, but the lettering was too small to read from a distance. But somehow Miles already knew what it would say before he got there.

***Su Vin***
***Family owned and operated***
***Est. 1996***
***Hours of operation: 10:00 a.m. to 6:00 p.m. daily***

This is fate, he told himself, because it was and because it had to be. Because it made a terrible sort of sense that the one place he'd avoided for the past eight years would be the place that now held the answers he sought.

Miles turned down the main drive of the public entrance to the winery. There was a sepia glow to the afternoon sun. It lit up the leaves on the trees like daylight stars, and everything felt burnt around the edges. Miles kept walking and walking, and no one stopped him. He walked past the tasting room and the sales office. He slipped into the fields on the north side of the property.

He knew where he was going.

*Exactly.*

It was late season, postharvest, and most of the grapes were gone.

All that remained were reedy brown vines wrapped around wire, a sight that made his heart squeeze with mourning. Sad, it was sad not to see life growing. When Miles reached the muddy creek bed, he headed east. His shoes sank and squelched with each step.

From there it didn't take long.

The underground bunker had been built on what was now an untended portion of the property, behind the rotting hulk of the vineyard's first pressing machine. It was hidden from sight due to the way shade from the neighboring oak trees fell, and the fact that crab and timothy grass had grown up and over the bunker doors. As Miles approached, he saw that someone had thrown a chain around the whole thing to keep strangers from crawling down there.

*Or to keep people in.*

His legs trembled.

Maybe he couldn't go through with this.

*Go,* the wind whispered, *go go go go,* and Miles glanced behind him. Then above. The sky was melting, rays of color dripping through the clouds like light refracted from a prism being held underwater.

Miles bent and took a rock to the rusted padlock. It fell away easily. His fingers worked and tugged the chain, pulling the links free. He tossed the whole thing into the grass, then sat back on his haunches.

Sweat ran down his face. It stung his scrapes and bruises from where he'd been hit, and the saltiness dripped into his mouth. Miles stared at the double doors that lay in the ground.

*(Dorothy doors)*

Was this it then? Was this the moment he'd seen in his vision? That bloody scene of sacrifice and pain? A whimper lodged in his throat, because Miles wasn't sure he was ready for the end, for this all to be over. He just felt *so scared.* But then the words from the Bible his mother would read to him when he was tiny and ill and sick in bed tumbled through his mind like a lullaby. *Go; behold, I send you out as lambs in the midst of wolves,* she'd say, and that's when Miles remembered that suffering could have a purpose. That *he* could have a purpose, too. So he reached with both arms and yanked opened the bunker doors.

A rush of cold air hit him. It smelled like spiders. He stood on the edge of the cement stairs that led down into the blackness, and a rare shudder of surety ran through him because he suddenly knew. He *knew*.

Sometimes to end things, you had to go back to the beginning.

Only it wasn't his end he was facing.

It didn't have to be.

With this revelation, both freeing and true, a puff of fear floated from his shoulders, like the tiniest spark of earthly magic. Miles stood tall as he took his first step into the dark cellar. Then the next. He kept going and going, descending deep into the earth.

*Wolves to the lamb,* the wind whispered as it followed, swirling at his feet in its twisting, taunting way.

But sometimes, he whispered back, "Lambs to the wolf."

# *chapter twenty-eight*

*Where was Miles?*

It was a different day but Emerson and May were spending the dwindling hours of their afternoon together again, this time at his apartment as a result of her inviting herself over. Emerson thought he was okay with that, for the most part—his mother was working late—but he had no idea where his brother was.

Which was both weird and totally normal.

"Do you ever go to his grave?" May asked. She was standing by the desk in the room he shared with Miles, and her eyes were sad.

He'd been telling her about his father. About how he'd died and how he missed him.

"Nah. Not really. My mom doesn't like to go. Last time I went I was thirteen. I went by myself after school one day, and I got really angry. Told him I hated him and everything. Stupid. It was stupid of me." Emerson felt twitchy, which meant words were spilling from his mouth like air. He liked having her here, he really did, but he couldn't stop thinking about the fact that his apartment was gross. And claustrophobic. And didn't have air conditioning. And smelled like bad pizza, thanks to the restaurant next door. It was hard to relax with those kinds of thoughts spiraling through his head. She'll see through me, he thought. She'll read my mind.

She'll *know.*

Only May didn't seem to know. That was the thing. She had no idea. She just walked around and touched a few items that were on Miles's side of the room, running her finger along a stack of books, including a worn copy of *Watership Down* and a tattered paperback titled *Microbe Hunters.* She paused to inspect an old charcoal drawing of dead birds, something Miles had done as a child and hung on the wall but had never taken down. It was creepy as hell, and Emerson asked him once what it was about.

"I saw it," Miles said dreamily. "I saw it in my head, and it came true."

Emerson turned his attention back to May, steeped in the way her presence pooled around the room like liquid. The way the fading sun lit her skin with a rosy glow. It was like she was from another century. Another world.

"What was he like, your dad?" she asked.

"He was a good guy. That's why I was so mad, I guess. But I mean, he could be kind of a hardass, too, sometimes."

"Were you close?"

"Sure. Sort of. I mean, my brother was really tight with him. I'm more of a mama's boy. But my dad, he was outgoing, you know? That's what I remember most. Always wanted to tell you everything when he was really into something. Like cars. Or horse racing. Or brewing beer. Once it was snowflakes."

"Snowflakes?"

Emerson nodded, then sat down on his own bed. Wiped his hands on his jeans. "Miles had this book when we were kids, and our dad used to read it to us. Over and over. It was about this guy a long time ago who set out to photograph snowflakes. He wanted to prove that they were all different, you know? Unique. But I guess it's not an easy thing to do, taking pictures of snow. Especially back then, with those old cameras: they got hot, melted all the flakes. But this guy was obsessed. He dedicated his whole life to the snowflakes, spent all his money on different equipment, just to get those images. Just to prove they existed."

"What happened to him?"

He shrugged. "I don't remember. I think he got pneumonia and died."

"That's depressing, Emerson."

"Most things about my dad are. In hindsight, at least."

"My cousin killed herself," May said. "Last year."

He looked up at her, at the shadows falling across her lovely face. "I'm sorry. That sucks."

"She was only twenty-two. She wanted to be a doctor, and she'd just gotten into med school. Harvard."

"Jesus."

"I know. She took a bunch of pills when she knew her parents weren't going to be home. They live out in Illinois, near Chicago. Her mom was the one who found her. The thing is, her family got the coroner to say it was an accidental overdose on her death certificate. Because they were embarrassed, I guess. Or ashamed. But I know she did it on purpose."

Emerson shivered. *Ashamed.* He hated that word. To him, it brought up images of red-faced kids and scolding parents. Of his brother's own whipped-dog cower. But was shame the reason Emerson had been lied to about his father's suicide? Worse, was it the reason *he'd* never asked anyone about it, even after he'd found out the truth?

"How do you know she did it on purpose?" he asked May.

"I know because she'd tried before. She told me about it the last time we saw each other. She'd taken pills twice, and they didn't work. She even told me why. But I didn't tell anyone. And now . . . now I can't tell." She turned and met his gaze. "You're the first person I've talked to about it, actually."

Emerson got up from the bed and walked over to her. Put his head on her shoulder. Held her close.

She stroked his back.

"Don't hate your dad, Em," she whispered. "He made a mistake doing what he did, and he can't ever take that back. It's a sad thing, the not being able to take it back. It's the worst."

He kissed her.

Ten minutes later they were on his bed fooling around. Her skirt was up and his jeans were down, and Emerson wasn't worried anymore about the heat or the pizza smell or how claustrophobic his room was. He thought maybe this was it, and she was his, and all the things he'd been worried about really weren't that important in the grand scheme of things. Wrong was wrong, sure, but if no one knew about the wrong thing he'd done, what was the harm?

But then May had to go and say, "So did Sadie send you those pictures?"

And Emerson went from feeling turned on to feeling like the worst person in the world. The kind of guy who'd stopped caring when his little brother got sick or hurt, because he was sick and hurt all the time. The kind of guy who used the girl he liked in ways that demeaned her. The kind of guy who cut the legs off frogs and the heads off birds and—

"She doesn't have any damn pictures," he muttered under his breath.

"What was that?"

"No," he said. "Not yet."

"She's funny, that girl. Her sense of humor is dry."

"I didn't know Sadie had a sense of humor."

"Oh, she does. She makes me laugh. Did you know her dad makes documentaries? From all over the world. We watched one in history last year. It was about Huaorani teenagers."

"I don't like her," Emerson said plainly, and more than anything, he wanted to kiss May on the mouth again and have her kiss him back, but now the guilt was spilled between them, like an ocean. And he still couldn't swim.

"Em?" she said.

"Yeah?"

"Why me?"

He stared at her. "What?"

May lay on her back, arms stretched above her head as she stared at the ceiling, which was made of that terrible popcorn material, all gaudy and cheap, dotted with specks of fake gold. "I was wondering why you liked me. Other girls like you, you know. You play sports. You could have anyone. Some cute blond cheerleader, maybe."

"Forget blond cheerleaders. I like you. You're prettier, anyway."

"Oh, come on. White guys don't think like that."

Emerson's heart beat faster. What did she mean? She *was* prettier. That was the truth. Cheerleaders were girls like Trish Reed, beauty marred by pettiness and snobbery. Besides, desire wasn't about thinking. It was about *wanting*. What you couldn't have. What you were driven to conquer. "Well, maybe those other guys, maybe they're racist or something."

"Oh, hush." May turned and pressed a finger to his lips. "Everyone's racist. Me, you, everybody. That's just how it is."

"You really believe that?"

"I know that. It's the world we live in. And knowing *that's* the only way to change things. Pretending to be something you're not's the worst, don't you think? If all the pretending does is trick you into believing you're different than who you really are."

Emerson didn't answer. Maybe it was the world they lived in—his own mom proved that fact—but he didn't think it was up to him to change things. That was something other people did. People who cared. People who wanted to be remembered for their actions.

May moved her finger down from his lips, running it along his jaw, his neck, his chest. "But there are white guys out there who make a fetish out of being with girls like me, you know? The blacker the berry, the sweeter the juice. I don't like that. I don't want you to want me that way."

"I don't want you that way. I mean, maybe I am racist or something. Hell, I don't know. I've definitely done things in my past that I'm not proud of. But what you said, about a fetish, that's not how I feel."

"Good," she said, smiling.

"The sweeter the juice?" he asked.

"So I've heard."

"Is it true?"

"That's for you to find out," she said. Then, "Actually, it doesn't taste that sweet to me. More salty."

Emerson's jaw dropped. "You've tasted it?"

May blushed. "I mean, just myself, you know. I was curious."

"I'm curious, too," he said, which was true. He was very curious. But he was also relieved that he now had a way to give to May without taking. He still owed her, didn't he? After what he'd done. He owed her and he wanted them to be even, so he pushed her gently on her back, and he gave and gave and gave.

But the whole time, while he was busy doing all that guilty giving, Emerson couldn't help thinking, *Where's Miles? He should definitely be home by now.*

*Where the hell could he be?*

# *part 3*

## The Hunter

"Sometimes I think evil is a tangible thing—with wave lengths, just as sound and light have."

—Richard Connell,
*The Most Dangerous Game*

# *chapter twenty-nine*

Sadie,

Here are thirteen facts about my relationship with Charlie Burns:

1. Our fathers served together in the Marines.
2. We were roommates fall semester of our freshman year. This was at Charlie's request. He didn't want to be friendless when he got to Rothshire.
3. I have Tourette syndrome. Maybe you knew that. Maybe you

didn't. I never told you. It's a lot better than it used to be and if people don't figure it out on their own, it's not something I like to bring up.

4. Charlie knew.
5. He called me a defect and a freak and a fucking retard for the entire five months we lived together.
6. I took it, and I laughed at every single joke he made at my expense.
7. Some of my tics I try only to do in private. They're embarrassing.
8. Charlie knew that, too. He set up a camera in our room and filmed me and showed it to everyone at school.
9. He got suspended.
10. I changed rooms.
11. He blamed me for the suspension and never let up. All year he harassed me in various ways, including, but not limited to, attacking me in the gym locker room, pulling my shorts down, and telling everyone I had a small dick.
12. I spent most of the summer between freshman and sophomore year being treated for anxiety and depression.
13. Sophomore year I met you.

—R

Dumpster Boy didn't show up in fencing class the next day. Or the day after that. He didn't show up anywhere, according to the talking heads on all the local news stations and the voicemail left by the school district superintendent.

Fifteen-year-old Miles Tate had vanished.

It happened on Wednesday, precisely two days after he was beat up on the street and left for dead by some unidentified boys, and precisely five days after he was hospitalized for a seizure of unknown origin. The last place he'd been seen was his math class, where he'd asked to use the restroom and never returned. The mystery surrounding his middle-of-the-day disappearance stirred a whirlwind of rumors, as did the fact that no one really knew him. Miles was described by everyone—classmates, teachers, neighbors, total strangers—as a quiet kid, a loner, a bullying victim, and, possibly, as the most salacious rumors went, an abused child. He'd run away, they said. He'd been kidnapped. He'd been murdered. He'd had a brain hemorrhage and died alone. He'd been taken by space aliens or hit by a train. Sadie didn't know him well enough to disagree with any of this, except the space alien thing because that was just fucking stupid, and seriously, why would they take *him*? But she hated the way they talked about Dumpster Boy on the news. It made her cheeks puff up and her head spin with thoughts of violence, because they talked about him like he was an object of pity, not a real person who was sad and screwed up, but also unique, the way a snowflake was: beautiful and strange and complex when you saw it up close, no matter how much you resented the fact that it was falling from the damn sky and ruining your whole day.

Miles was also Emerson Tate's little brother. Sadie knew that now, too. Clearly there was some weird shit floating around in the Tate gene pool. And while she couldn't conjure up any more of a memory of young Miles, just that brief flash of a waifish child, clinging to the legs of his mother like a parasite, all the connections between the three of them felt complicated in the same way that Roman's emails to Sadie felt complicated.

Sadie *hated* that. Complications. They were so useless, the way they made things seem important through mere coincidence or connection. Sadie didn't believe in finding meaning in things if the meaning wasn't obvious. The truth didn't get to be what you made of it. It just *was*. Anyone who believed otherwise reminded her of the hormonally challenged American girls at her Parisian boarding school, the ones with the blue eyes and the trust funds, who liked to look her up and down when they heard her last name and ask "but where are you *from*?" when Sadie said she was American, too. They were the ones who forever blathered on with pointless stories about how they *just missed getting into a car accident, by like,* <u>a second</u> and *wasn't that* <u>wild</u>*?* and *didn't things like that, like, really make you* <u>think</u>*?*

People like that didn't understand there was no *almost* when it came to fate.

People like that were ones Sadie knew she could lie to and get away with it.

Always.

When Sadie first met Emerson Tate, however, she didn't lie. She was nine and he was ten, and she had no reason to. If anything, *he* was the one who lied, even if he didn't know it. But she knew things about him even before his mother had shown up to tend to Sadie's maternal grandfather, who was dying of brain cancer in the bedroom right next door to Sadie's. *Her* mom had had to give up her duties at the winery she'd founded in order to care for him, because her deadbeat brothers couldn't be bothered to help. They were too busy tending to their polo games and budding alcoholism. Hiring a hospice nurse should've been a good thing, considering, but Sadie's dad had done it without asking first. That meant serious fallout in the Su household. The revelation that he was bringing in one with children had set off a ground war.

"He's my father," her mother hissed. "My father hates children. All of them. And you know what? So do I."

Sadie's father had been firm. "She's excellent. And she needs the work. She's Mark's widow, L. They need help. God knows we can afford to give it."

"But why the boys?"

"They have nowhere else to go. But they'll be fine here. Plenty of room for kids to play and stay out of your way. I promise. Plus Sadie will help keep them busy, isn't that right?" He'd looked over to where she stood in the kitchen doorway, watching them closely.

Sadie gave a quick shrug, small shoulders grazing her pigtails. "Maybe Grandpa will die soon so they'll go away faster."

Her mom had fled the room then, crying, and her father crouched down on his knees and beckoned her over.

Sadie went to him, dancing into his arms. That champagne thrill of victory bubbled inside of her.

"That wasn't nice," he told her sternly. His hands smelled of cigar smoke and fresh rosemary from the garden.

"I wasn't trying to be nice," she shot back.

"I understand that. But you know, a famous priest once said, 'The things that we love tell us what we are.' "

"So?"

"You love cruelty, Sadie. That's not a good thing."

She'd twisted in his grasp. Pinched at his neck and left a mark.

"I mean it," he said. "You can't live this way, hurting people the way you do. I won't let you."

"Who's Mark?" she asked. "What happened to him?"

Her father's eyes grew soft, sad. "Mark Tate. He used to work on my car. He was the nicest guy. Had his troubles, but he was a real family man. He died last fall."

"How?"

"Do you know what suicide is? Do you know what that word means?"

"Yes. It's what Iris Chang did. She shot herself in her car. Pop pop pop."

He tightened his jaw. "How do you know about that?"

"I heard you talking about it on the telephone. You wanted to make a film about her. So that's what this Mark did? He shot himself?"

"Not exactly. But he died in his car. And his kids . . . I don't think they're taking it very well. One of them, especially. He's sort of in denial about it all. His mother's worried, and she's already got enough to be worried about. So be kind to the boys, Sadie. How you treat them will tell me what you are."

The next day, the widowed nurse and her two boys had showed up at the house, right on time. The nurse, whose name was Gracie Tate, spent the afternoon doing things like ordering medical supplies, administering pain medication to Sadie's grandfather, and changing his catheter. For all her tears and endless complaining, this allowed Sadie's mother to lie down and drink wine, although not necessarily in that order.

Sadie crept around the house that first day, shadowing the nurse. She mostly did this to see the catheter thing happen. Sadie longed to know what a penis looked like in real life, and she also longed to touch one. But when she caught a glimpse of her grandfather's, it reminded her of a horrible slug or a turd that had been left out in the sun, and she quickly decided she'd look elsewhere for that opportunity.

It didn't take long for Sadie to figure out which of the boys was the screwed-up one. This boy was surly and mean, and had the pretty lips and blond curls of an angel. Sadie watched as he stole one of her grandfather's watches, sprinkled weed killer on a patch of new-growth Riesling vines, and put laxatives in the cat's food bowl so that it shit all over the living room carpet and tracked it around the house, including Sadie's room. He also managed to push his brother down a flight of stairs when he thought no one was looking, and insisted on using racial slurs whenever he addressed any of the vineyard workers. She found this both ironic and cowardly, seeing as his own mother was hired help and the boy never dared say anything about Sadie's immigrant father. Not once.

After school one day, she trailed the boy around the property and out to the boggy creek. She crawled up a tree and lay on her belly in the branches while he picked up rocks and looked beneath them. After a few tries, he captured a small green frog, cupping it in his hands before pinning it to the ground and cutting its legs off with a switchblade.

The frog lay dying, and Sadie watched as thc boy shoved both hands down the front of his shorts. He was doing something strange and urgent in there when she called out to him. And she didn't lie. She told him the honest truth about himself.

"Bad," she told him brightly. "You're a bad person."

# *chapter thirty*

When Emerson had been in the eighth grade, his computer programming teacher had stood before the class one day and announced that he had a foolproof method to get people to stop smoking.

"It's simple, and it's guaranteed to work," he told them, as he leaned against the plywood lectern positioned at the front of the room. "Every time a smoker has a craving for a cigarette, all that person needs to do is tell themselves that they can have one, in exactly one hour."

Of course everyone in the room had raised their hands and opened their mouths and asked how anybody could quit smoking if they never stopped. But Emerson understood right away. The point was that if you followed the teacher's instructions to a T, you'd never light up again. You could become a nonsmoker without ever committing to stopping. Behavior was what mattered.

The mind would follow.

That's how it was with Miles's disappearance. To Emerson, it felt as if he'd traveled someplace frightening and foreign without even realizing he was in motion. It started when Miles didn't come home for dinner Wednesday evening. That wasn't so strange, considering, and besides, it was also the afternoon May had come over and taught Emerson that the greatest gift a girl's body had to give was indeed more saline than sweet. Dazed and spent and helplessly lost in the promise of her goodness, he hadn't noticed the hours passing until it was almost ten and still, there was no sign of Miles. He wasn't answering his phone, but he kept the damn thing switched off half the time or let it run out of juice. And why not? It wasn't like he was waiting for anyone to call.

So Emerson had gone to sleep, only to wake the next morning and realize Miles still wasn't there. Or maybe he'd come and left early, the way Miles often did. Emerson didn't want to freak out his mother or cause a whole episode, so he went to school like normal and asked for the desk lady at the front office to page Miles.

But he didn't show up. Not to the office. Not to any of his classes. Not anywhere.

Even then, there was no defining moment or flashbulb of awareness, just a gradual accumulation of absence. More hours and more doubt and more questions added up until over a whole day had passed and still, nobody knew where his brother was. Emerson braced himself and called his mom, and together they went down to the police station to report what was already so very, very obvious.

Miles was gone.

---

The cops stopped by their apartment again and again as the hours ticked by. They asked the same questions each time they came, along with the occasional new ones. Had they heard from him? Had they heard anything? Did they ever see him with anybody? Did he do drugs? Did he sell drugs? Did anyone in the house do drugs? He really didn't have *any* friends?

It was Detective Gutierrez who knocked on the door early Friday morning as dawn crept into town. Emerson waved her in with a yawn. He hadn't slept all night. He couldn't. His mind, his whole body, felt jumpy and dark.

"My mom's in her room," he whispered. "The doctor made her take a pill. I could try and wake her, though."

"No, don't do that." The detective stayed on the stoop. "How's she doing, Emerson?"

He shook his head. "Not good."

"We're working as hard as we can."

"I know."

"Do you think you and I could talk for a little bit?"

"About what?"

"About Miles. And . . . your mother."

Something bubbled in Emerson's gut. Hot and bitter. As if some stove burner of emotion flickering beneath him had just been turned up.

"Sure," he said. "Let's go outside."

Detective Gutierrez nodded, and she waited while he grabbed a key and stepped out, pulling the front door shut behind him. The morning air was chill and fresh, and Emerson breathed in deeply as they walked out to the parking lot to stand beneath the redwood trees that shaded the complex from the road.

"What did you want to talk about?" he asked.

"I know this might seem—"

"Don't screw around with me," he said. "Just tell me what you have to say. I know it's not anything good or you wouldn't have brought me out here."

The detective nodded, meeting his gaze with those sharp, steely eyes of hers. "Five years ago your mother was arrested for suspicion of child abuse and child endangerment."

"And those charges were dropped."

"True. But the suspicions were raised after your brother made multiple trips to the ER for different physical ailments."

"So? He's not a strong kid. He's got all sorts of allergies. That's not exactly a criminal act. But him getting sick so easily, it's exactly why you guys need to find—"

"Last week your brother was in the ER again."

Emerson folded his arms. "What's your point?"

"My point is that it kind of raises suspicions again."

"Isn't it more suspicious that *this week* Miles got beat up by a bunch of asshole kids running around the streets of Sonoma?"

"Did he?" she asked.

*"What?"*

"You heard me."

The bubbling inside Emerson turned up. Way up. A full-boiled rage. "Unbelievable. This is unbelievable. My mother has *nothing* to do with this."

"Well, we can't find the boys who beat him up. There were no witnesses, and Miles wouldn't tell us anything."

"That's not my mom's fault! Just . . ." His voice cracked. "Just find my brother. *Please.*"

"We're trying. I promise you that." She reached out to touch his shoulder, but Emerson flinched. Sidestepped out of her reach.

"Fuck your promises," he snarled. "And fuck you!" He stalked off, didn't look back. He marched up the stairs and went inside the apartment. Slammed the door behind him. He tried talking himself down by standing outside his mother's bedroom, which was a joke. Like he'd ever been able to shield her from anything.

Emerson sank to the floor in the darkened hallway. Put his head in his hands. Tried to tamp down his roiling emotions. It hurt too much, thinking, feeling. He shouldn't have lost his temper with the cop, he *knew* that, but he just wanted this all to end. To be over. For Miles to come back and for things to be how they were.

That was it. That wasn't too much to ask.

Was it?

# *chapter thirty-one*

Theory #3: The Most Dangerous Game

I know you know the story because you called me Rainsford once, like you saw some of him in me. Or maybe you saw yourself in General Zaroff. Whichever it was, Connell's story's one I reread recently, and I was struck by something I hadn't noticed before. I'm guessing it's one of those questions that doesn't come with the teacher's discussion guide when it's taught in high school English, because it's so obvious to people who aren't me. But here's what I noticed: Zaroff and Rainsford are both hunters. Rainsford is set up to be different because of his ethical boundaries; he won't hunt men. But by the end, Zaroff and Rainsford aren't actually different at all because Rainsford is pushed to cross the same ethical line he condemns Zaroff for crossing by killing him in cold blood. I get that it's a story about perspective, about how what looks like madness or evil from one vantage point can look like righteousness when you're standing somewhere else.

But is the assumption that, deep down, we're all capable of murder? That we only hold those impulses back due to moral vanity and for no other reason?

Sometimes I feel like that's truly the world we live in, and I'm the only one who doesn't understand the rules. Everyone else is walking close to the cliff's edge, peering down at the bloody ground below, trying to guess who's going to get pushed over next. Meanwhile, I'm the one clinging to the wall, too broken with grief over those who've already been lost.

I guess what I'm saying is I know that you're Zaroff and I know you're Rainsford, and maybe that's the answer. Maybe that's humanity in a nutshell, rather than that hamster wheel bullshit you tried to spin me. The thing is, I'm not playing the same game as the rest of you. In my heart of hearts, I know I'd choose death at the hands of Ivan the giant rather than risk becoming the hunter. Every single time. Maybe Father Carson would let me believe there's nobility in that choice, which is the kindness I find in my faith, but even I know there's no grace in fear. My life is not a life of sacrifice or martyrdom.

My life is maddening.

—R

P.S. Why did you want to know about Charlie Burns?

I wanted to know about Charlie because of a boy here that I met. He reminded me of you and he got beat up by some guys, only he wouldn't say who did it. I guess I wondered if something similar happened with you and Charlie. And it did. And maybe I guess I also wondered if that was part of why this boy and I got to know each other. Because of you. Or me. Or something. I don't know.

What happened to him?

What do you mean? Why are you asking me that?

You're using the past tense to talk about him.

Yeah, well, he's missing. He disappeared.

Missing how?

I don't know how. He's just gone. He left school on Wednesday and no one's seen him since. That's two days now. He's only fifteen.

You're worried about him, aren't you?

No. Yes. I guess.

That's interesting.

Why?

I didn't think you cared about other people.

I don't. I mean, I'm kind of fucked up right now. But he's a sad kid, R. I don't know. He might be really screwed up.

Like me.

Yes, like you.

Then you should know where to look.

I should?

Absolutely.

Hey, how come you keep sending me your weird theories? It's stupid, you know. It's not going to change anything.

Because you still haven't told me why.

Sadie put her phone away before she said something else to Roman. Something she'd regret. She was sitting on her ass in the dying sun, half-buried in the dry earth of the southern hillside of her family's vineyard, and she was drunk. It was a lazy stupid kind of drunk, the kind that made her mind move slowly and her mouth taste like vomit.

All around her, the air smelled fetid. The natural decay process of the grapevines had been interrupted by this sudden shift in temperature. Instead of heading into the cool fog days of autumn and signaling to the plants that it was time to go fallow, this freak October heat wave was melting everything into a rancid soup. Not to mention there was a fire burning. It was many miles away, out in the Central Valley, but smoke and ash filled the landscape with an apocalyptic haze.

This hazy shit-smelling place was Sadie's escape. Her sanctuary. How gross was that? There was still no news about Miles, and she'd come out here to read that rambling message from Roman because her insensitive bitch of a mom had invited guests over to the house, some sort of late-season dinner party. Like the town wasn't already in the midst of a tragedy. A kid was *missing*. A kid their family had known. But life went on for the wealthy and uncouth, and the party was a whole fancy thing involving cocktail dresses and sunset views and assholes who threw around words like *charcuterie* and *aperitif* and *ménage a trois*. Sadie figured if she had to spend any time with those people, she was liable to puke, burn the place to the ground, or commit mass murder. Maybe all three.

So she'd taken her phone and a bottle of the most expensive champagne she could find and dragged herself out here, careful to skirt around the back creek and the old press and the abandoned cellar, places that reminded her of Emerson Tate and the twisted things they used to do together. Those were memories she didn't need at the moment. Not ever probably.

Sadie guzzled down the last of the champagne and stared out at the valley and the homes and everything she hated. A soft twinkling to the east told her someone had set floating candles free in her family's pool. She groaned. Floating candles had to be one of the worst party decorations ever invented, what with their fake romantic pretension and atmospheric contrivance. In terms of general tackiness, they ranked right up there with wind puppets and those bags of Jordan almonds that got handed out at weddings.

The malaise and ennui running through Sadie's brain took on strength, made her long to do something bad. Something hurtful. Maybe this was what Roman's Tourette's thing was like. Being filled to the rim with the burning need to *act*.

More than anything, Sadie ached to be elsewhere. Anywhere. In a different body. A different life. This patch of vineyard hillside was the exact spot her father had gotten mad at her once. Sadie had said something mean to her mother, who said something mean back, and

Sadie threw a rock at her legs before turning and running as fast as she could.

Like a greyhound after a hare, her father had chased her down in the rows of grapes, scooping her up to lay her across his lap. It was the only time he'd ever spanked her, and while he'd done it, he told her:

*This. Is. For. Your. Own. Good.*

And maybe it had been.

Only now Sadie's father was gone, long gone, and with something like the bough-snap pain of first heartbreak, she was beginning to understand that he wouldn't be coming back.

Ever.

But with Miles, there was still hope.

Wasn't there?

The thing about Roman and what happened between them wasn't that he'd wanted a friend when she hadn't wanted friends. And it wasn't that he'd wanted to be something more than friends when she hadn't wanted that either. Both of those things were true, of course, but they were on him. Sadie knew that. She'd read *Venus in Furs*. If the boy wanted to be punished, then he must like the punishment.

Or else he believed he deserved it.

But after that awkward autumn afternoon in his dorm room, that day he'd so clearly wanted her, and when she'd so clearly rejected him, Sadie made the choice to push him away. Not because she'd wanted him to leave, but because it felt good to push.

*Really* good.

"You're pathetic," she told him on their next walk through the woods, with the smell of wood smoke mingling with the chilled promise of winter to come.

"How's that?" he'd asked, but kept his brown eyes cast downward, watching his own feet move forward, like he couldn't believe what they were doing. Like they were betraying him by following her.

"It's like, we all have this place in the world. Somewhere we can run on our hamster wheels and be comfortable. There are TV shows to watch. Books to read. Music to listen to. People to spend time with, maybe even fuck every now and then. There's something and someone for everyone. So we can go through life and protect ourselves from discomfort, from having our beliefs challenged, and blissfully ignore the rest of the big bad world that's out there. It's what most of us do. Hell, no one really wants to take a stand or answer any call to action if they don't have to. We just say we do to feel better about ourselves. For most people, though, life is about finding their hamster wheel and running on it. It gives the illusion of progress. Not that things are perfect, nothing ever is, but there's a sweet spot of peace out there, so long as there's food on the table and we don't have bombs blowing up around us or something.

"But there are some people who find comfort in discomfort. In knocking people out of their hamster wheels and setting them free onto the four-lane highway of reality. Look at Sartre. Look at Kierkegaard. Remember what he said? 'The crowd is untruth.' Kierkegaard knew. And people like that, like us, we're the ones the hamsters should fear. Because other people's fear, it kind of gets us off."

# *chapter thirty-two*

By Friday afternoon the story about Miles had shifted. Emerson felt it happen the way he felt a storm brewing off the ocean or the earth rumble beneath his feet; it was in his bones and in his soul—a swirling sea change in interest, in urgency.

And still, Miles was missing.

The change had something to do with the school psychologist who'd talked to Miles after he'd gotten beaten up. Emerson didn't know what the psychologist had said, exactly, but the whispers of rumors that rode through town were no longer *abducted, beaten, left for dead, killed by his own mom*. Instead they became rumors that Miles had taken his own life. That he'd been suicidal. Or homicidal. And weren't those really the same thing?

Hope and desperation faded from the public eye, leaking into smug validation like air deflating from a balloon with a hiss, not a pop.

*Depressed kid. Never saw him smile.*

*Dad did it. Now the boy did it, too. Damn shame.*

*Those things run in the family, you know.*

*Mom is crazy. No wonder.*

*Probably queer. He looked queer.*

*Meth'll do that . . .*

*Need to drag the river.*

*Check the train tracks.*

*Look in the woods. I'll bet you anything he did it in the woods.*

*She even told me why. . . .*

The day May told him about it, Emerson hadn't bothered asking *why* her Harvard-bound cousin had taken pills and killed herself at the age of twenty-two, when she had her whole shining life ahead of her. He hadn't asked because it didn't seem like he had the right to know. And now he couldn't ask, he realized, because by asking, it might break him. He just might fall apart for good to see the sweet, sweet sorrow in her eyes. Her pained reflection of grief. Everything wonderful got ruined eventually.

By guilt.

By *him*.

Had that moment at the party been the tipping point? Is that where it had all started to fall apart? Miles had been lying in a hospital recovering from his seizure while Emerson had been at Trish Reed's, up in that lonely bathroom with May. She'd passed out while he was looking at her, just rolled those pretty brown eyes shut, and then he couldn't *stop* staring. At her body. Her face. At how still she was. Just barely breathing. After that, it'd been such a simple thing to do. To unzip his jeans, to reach down to—

Emerson got to his feet abruptly. Told his mom he needed air. A lie, but a necessary one. Once outside in the smothering afternoon heat, he got into his car and drove right out of town. He headed south, which was where the famous Sonoma Raceway was located, along with the auto repair shop where his dad had worked up until his death. And while no one at Brewster's Classic Cars & Automotive Care had ever crewed for NASCAR or IndyCar or even set a tire on the neighboring racetrack in any official capacity, Emerson's father told him once that *proximity mattered.*

"Listen to me, Em. Being close to greatness makes a difference. It just does. You date the prettiest girl or sit with the most popular kid at school, people start believing there's something special about you. After a while, you might start believing it, too. That's when you know a little bit of their shine is yours now."

The owner, Paul Brewster, stood outside the red brick building with a hose, washing down the flagstone patio where customers liked to wait in the sun while their cars were being serviced. He did a double take of recognition as the Mustang nosed in. Then he nodded and waved Emerson forward, pointing for him to park by a wine barrel planter filled with sprawling vines and some sort of purple flower.

By the time Emerson unbuckled himself and got out, Brewster was already running his hand along the Mustang's hood. His gray eyes were misty, like a watercolor gone bad, and he pulled Emerson into an awkward embrace before stepping back and gazing down at the car again.

"How's she running?" he asked.

"Pretty good."

"You're leaking oil."

"I know."

"Suspension's dragging, too. And I bet that air filter needs changing."

"It does."

"Better bring her in sometime, okay? Let me look at her."

"I will," Emerson said firmly, although they both knew he wouldn't. He couldn't afford to.

Brewster nodded again. Touched the hood with scarred fingers that were as long and slender as the rest of him. He'd been one of Emerson's father's oldest friends. They'd grown up together. Emerson's dad always said he'd looked up to Brewster like a big brother.

*But that's not the way Miles looks at me.*

"Why'd he do it?" Emerson blurted out.

Brewster squinted at him. "Who?"

"My dad. I want to know why."

"That why you're here? To talk about that?"

"Yeah. Well, Miles is missing and I think maybe he had some real, you know, mental issues. Now they're saying . . . now they're saying he might have—" Emerson couldn't finish the sentence. He just shook his head.

"Ah, shit." Brewster's face fell. "Shit. That's terrible. Just terrible. Miles was always such a sweet kid. Tenderhearted, you know? I was hoping he had just run away. That he'd come home when he was ready."

"Maybe that *is* what happened," Emerson said, thinking of his own heart, which was anything but tender. "But if what they're saying, if it's true, it'll kill my mom. It really will."

"I'm sorry. I'm so sorry."

"Look, if there's something about my dad that you can tell me, *anything,* maybe it'll help me find Miles. That's why I'm here. I don't know what else to do or who to talk to."

Brewster blew air through his cheeks, rolled his neck side to side. There were tiny pockets of red in his eyes, like maybe he hadn't slept in a while. "I miss your dad every day. Every goddamn day. But it's not a simple thing, talking about Mark, about what happened to him."

Nothing *happened,* Emerson thought darkly. It wasn't some passive thing. His father did exactly what he set out to do. "Tell me what you know. Tell me anything."

"Let's go to my office."

Emerson followed him toward the back of the garage. The raw scent of motor oil and coolant filled his nostrils and brought waves of memories flooding back: the hours he spent here as a young boy, crawling through the bays and stealing sips of beer from cans that had been left out; eavesdropping on the mechanics while they bitched about illegals coming to steal their jobs and girls they wanted to screw. Eventually, he and Miles had to stop coming because of some stupid liability issue, but until then, this place had been the one spot where Emerson had felt a little bit of independence. Of *freedom.*

"You look like him," Brewster said when they'd both sat down. "It's eerie."

"I know."

"You're taller, though. Probably got a good two inches on him."

"You think?"

"Absolutely," Brewster said. Then: "He didn't leave a note or anything, your dad. He just did it."

Emerson leaned forward in his chair, which was wood and squeaked beneath his weight. "The thing is, no one told me what he did when it happened. They just said he died. I guess I thought he'd had a heart attack or something. I don't know. I was a kid, and we didn't talk about it. We still don't talk about it. My mom, she's kind of fragile, you know? I had to find out what he'd done at *school.* From the girl whose dad arrested my mom. *She's* the one who told me he killed himself. Isn't that fucked up?"

Brewster gave him a funny look.

"What?" Emerson asked.

"That's not true."

"What's not true?"

"You were definitely told what happened to your father, Emerson. I know because I was there. Your mother had me come over and help the night Mark died. Shit, she was a real wreck. She didn't know what to do. None of us did. Your uncle was there, too. He and I sat you boys down, and we told you that your father had a sickness inside of him that made him do things he didn't want to do, and that this time his sickness made him kill himself. We told you what a terrible thing his sickness was because he wanted to live and because he loved you so very, very much, but that he'd died and wouldn't be coming back."

The back of Emerson's neck grew hot. Then hotter. "I don't remember that."

"Hardest damn thing I ever had to do."

"I seriously don't remember that."

"Well, I don't know what to say. I thought you understood. You seemed to. Miles, I couldn't tell, he was so little and scared, like a lost pup. But you reacted. At the time you were very . . ."

"Very what?"

"Angry," Brewster said.

Emerson took a deep breath. He felt sick. And dizzy. The night of his father's death was vivid and clear in his mind, all the tears, the confusion, his mother's wails. So why didn't he remember being told it was a suicide? Who could forget something like that?

"So he was depressed?" he managed.

"Sometimes, but it was more than that. Your dad, he was on the other end a lot."

"Other end?"

"Manic, you know." Brewster made a set of fluttering wings with his hands. The wings went up toward the ceiling in a shiver of shadows, before making a diving swoop for the floor. "He was impulsive. Always flying high before he came crashing down. He thought he could do anything when he was like that, but he didn't really think sometimes. That was the problem. Mark ruined a lot of relationships that way. Almost ruined ours more than once. And the one with your mom. They say it's a brain thing, chemicals out of balance, but he didn't ever want to hear that when he was up."

"You're saying my dad was bipolar or something? That's why he killed himself?"

"No, it's not *why*. Not directly, although it had to factor in somehow. But it was regret that did it, I think. All that guilt over things he'd done."

"Guilt for what?"

Brewster picked a pen up off his desk, a silver one. He spun it across his knuckles, around and around. Emerson's heart pounded. It was the same trick May had done in class the other day, before this whole nightmare with Miles had started.

*Before.*

"Let me ask you this," Brewster said, after a moment. "You ever done something you felt really terrible about? Something you shouldn't have, but that you can't take back?"

*yes oh yes*

*all the time, really*

"What kind of thing?" Emerson asked.

"Anything."

"Yeah, sure."

"Well, me, too. And I'm going to tell you my biggest regret because it's the only one I know, but I think it's important for you to hear about."

"Okay."

"Your dad came to me, maybe a week before he died. He was in real pain, after one of those crashes, and he asked me that same question. The one I just asked you. Only he followed it up with, 'how do you make it stop?' How do you make the guilt go away when it's eating you up inside? When you feel like you've let down the ones you love? At the time I was pissed. Some of the things he was doing, drinking, missing work, spending money he didn't have, it was hurting my business. Hurting *me.* So you know what I told him about getting rid of guilt?"

"What?"

Brewster's eyes went misty again. "I told him sometimes you don't deserve to."

Emerson drove to the town library after leaving Brewster's. He had to go somewhere. He couldn't face seeing his mom again so soon. Not with all the turmoil inside him. Not with all the questions chewing at his nerves.

He parked beneath a cypress tree, pulled the whisky bottle out from under the front seat, and let himself drink a little. The guilt was there, the way it always was, but Emerson kept on drinking. It didn't seem like adding more guilt on top of what was already inside him was going to matter too much at the moment. When he was done, he got out of the car, tossed the empty bottle into the bushes, and bounded up the steps to the stone building. He took them two at a time like the athlete he was and ignored the stares of the children and parents, who all surely knew his name and why his family was in the news these days.

Inside the library, a row of computers sat against the far wall, directly beneath a display of posters with information about registering to vote. *I should really do that,* Emerson thought. He was eighteen now. A damn adult. He ought to act like one.

He logged in to a computer with his city account and opened a web browser. He'd never been a big reader, but the library was where he'd spent a lot of time as a kid, especially in middle school, when they couldn't afford DSL payments. Here the internet was free, and unlike the school library, no one ever looked over his shoulder or restricted what sites he could visit.

Ducking his head over the keyboard, Emerson googled *bipolar disorder*. He'd heard of it, of course, but didn't know a lot about it, or about any mental disorders, really. He certainly didn't know his dad had had one, although it made sense, considering. Emerson's chest tightened. Was he about to find out that Miles was like their father, full of inner torment and destined to implode? Emerson clicked onto the first site that came up. He scanned the symptoms of mania, which included:

- Euphoria
- Grandiosity
- Pressured speech
- Racing thoughts
- Decreased need for sleep
- Increased sexual behavior
- Reckless use of drugs or alcohol
- Delusions or a break from reality (psychosis)

Emerson frowned. None of these sounded like Miles at all. Miles was gloomy and sickly and didn't talk to people if he could avoid it. No doubt, he fell more on the depressive side of things, although even that didn't seem quite right because the depression part didn't say anything about getting sick all the time and having to go to the hospital.

But reading over the manic symptoms again, a funny tickle grew in Emerson's throat. Like a laugh or some sort of rising sickness. Because Brewster didn't tell him that his father had died of euphoria or racing thoughts or even some kind of psychosis. It was *guilt* that killed him, Brewster had said. Along with the seasick sway of regret.

Two things Emerson knew a lot about.

Far more than he wanted to.

Far more than he should.

# chapter thirty-three

Sadie closed her eyes, made a nasty wish, and chucked the empty bottle of champagne straight over her shoulder, as hard as she could. Hand cupped to her ear, she waited for the clunk and crash of breaking glass.

But it never came.

Disappointed, she opened her eyes again. Got to her feet. And swayed. Everything about her felt sloshy, overfull, like she was on the verge of springing a leak. She lit a cigarette in order to keep herself grounded, then stumble-skidded down the hillside to retrieve the bottle. It deserved a more destructive end, she decided, and as she walked, Sadie sent one last impulsive email to Roman.

---

P.S. Is your dick really that small?

---

She made it to the dirt road that ran the perimeter of the property. Steeply cambered, it consisted of two parallel truck ruts that were the lowest points around. According to Newton's laws of motion and the theory of gravity, this stretch of road was precisely where the heavy champagne bottle should have rolled and lodged itself.

Only it wasn't here.

Sadie turned around and around. Peered through her sunglasses back up the hill. She couldn't see any point on the way down that the bottle might have gotten snagged or hung up on. Then she looked behind her and across the road into a bunch of scrub brush and wilted weeds.

No bottle.

What the hell? Sadie hated moments like this, when something she *knew* to be a fact was not, in fact, demonstrating its factness to her. It was just really fucking rude. She puffed harder on her cigarette, enjoying the burn on her windpipe and the hope that she was giving someone somewhere cancer. Ambling down the road a bit, she looked this way and that to see if the bottle might be caught in some funny shadow or a strange trick of the light. Nothing.

Then Sadie stopped walking. She blinked.

Up ahead, maybe an eighth of a mile farther and standing in the middle of the road perfectly upright, was the champagne bottle.

That did not make sense.

It just didn't.

Sadie walked faster, and now there was a cramp in her stomach, a tight one, right beneath her navel. She reached the bottle, leaned down, and picked it up. She held it to the light, turning it around and around, but there was nothing about the object that told her anything about its journey. Sadie considered the remote possibility that it had come down the side of the hill and rolled toward the road, only to be pushed far off course by a freak wind current, causing it to land in the most unlikely of positions—one of those brilliant oddities of nature only pure chance could produce, like the Hope Diamond or the Grand Canyon or even those Goblin Valley rock formations down in Utah that those dumbass Boy Scout leaders had gone and ruined.

Only there was no wind at the moment.

Not even a little bit.

The cramp in Sadie's stomach grew sharper.

Tucking the bottle beneath one arm, she veered toward the creek. It wasn't much farther, and once there, she could smash the bottle on the rocks by the water. That would make her feel better, more in control. If some of the pieces were large enough, she planned to lay them in the roadway and hope one of the vineyard workers got a flat. In particular, she had her sights set on Gerald Corning, who drove around in this shitty tricked-out Escalade with fuzzy dice hanging from the rearview mirror. As if Sadie's mom didn't already own his balls.

The old press was up ahead, on Sadie's right. A remnant from the vineyard's long-ago past, it was an ugly structure: a round slatted vat, framed by a thatched-roof structure that loomed from the earth like a monster. Beyond the press was the old wine cellar, also in disuse. This was the place Sadie and Emerson Tate had shared their darkest secrets during the months they'd spent together while his mom tended to Sadie's grandfather.

After seeing what he'd done with that frog, Sadie had invited him down with her and she'd shown him her collection of dead animals. Nothing she'd killed herself—Roman had been wrong about that. She might be a General Zaroff at heart, but not *literally.* The animals were mostly things she found while out exploring. She kept them hidden down in that dank room, to use when needed, like the time she'd dumped a handful of decomposing field mice into her uncle's custom leather riding boots after he told her parents she was an "insolent brat."

Pretty soon Sadie found out Emerson liked dead things, too, but for a very different reason. She didn't care much about his reasons; he could do what he wanted. But it was the last time she'd gone down there with him that she'd finally gotten to see a real penis and the things he could do with it.

"Aren't you supposed to look at naked ladies when you do that?" she'd asked from where she sat, legs dangling, on the marble-topped work slab that had once been used for corking. But Emerson wasn't looking at naked ladies. He wasn't even looking at her. In the dim glow of the bare lightbulb that hung and swayed from the dirt ceiling, he was doing what he was doing while staring down at the lifeless body of a small black cat he'd kept in his backpack all day before bringing it over after school. He told Sadie he'd found it already dead on the roadside, but she had her doubts. There were no tire marks on it or anything. The cat was just dead.

Dead. Dead. Dead.

And that's what he was looking at.

"I've never seen a naked lady," he grunted, before scrunching his face up in a funny way.

"Hmmph," said Sadie, as he made more faces. Later, in the privacy of her own room, she would touch herself once or twice after seeing what he did and how much he liked it, but nothing mind-blowing would happen, much to Sadie's bitter resentment. Not until she was older, at least. And then, it wasn't like what you read about in books or saw in movies; Sadie's body didn't *blossom* or *awaken* or *come of age* so much as it became *aware.* It wasn't all that different from learning how to wiggle her ears or getting her first period. She simply woke up one morning in her thirteenth year with a newfound sentience that taught her that *this* was what it was like to have fire in her veins, and *this* was how to bring her body alive with twisting want using the force of her own hand.

Dead cats weren't what she thought of then.

She glanced over toward where she knew the cellar lay. It was a spot that had been overrun with weeds and trash over the years, but she could usually make out the shape of the cement structure that had been poured into the earth to hold the double doors to the cellar.

Then Sadie frowned.

Because both the cellar doors were open.

Slowly, very slowly, the champagne bottle slipped from Sadie's armpit to smash onto the ground. Glass sprayed everywhere, across her feet, the dirt.

She barely noticed. She was already marching forward on tense legs, heading straight for the patch of overgrown grass and grubby weeds that sat in the shadow of the old press, and nothing felt right, not after finding the bottle in a place and a position it shouldn't have been, and now this.

The air hung in clumps all around her, small pockets of heat that she had to push through. It was an effort moving in such conditions, but she was determined to find out who was screwing around in a place no one should be. Sadie's dad had chained those cellar doors up years ago, just days before Emerson's mom was dismissed from her nursing job and Sadie's grandfather was transferred to a care hospital. He'd lingered there another month before falling out of bed and dying alone on the floor in the middle of the night.

When she was five yards from the cellar entrance, Sadie's phone chirped and all of her muscles loosened with relief. It was Roman, no doubt, and remembering what she'd asked him made her feel good again. It reminded her that she knew how to work people and get what she wanted out of them.

It was a reminder she seriously needed at the moment.

Sadie pulled her phone from her pocket, curious about his answer to her nosy question and wondering which way he would play it: seizing opportunity and demonstrating newfound bravado by telling her his dick was way bigger than she gave him credit for or maintaining his meekness, his gloomy honesty that was so Roman and so pathetic, because it seemed he hadn't yet realized that *everyone* lied about things like dick size and intelligence and their concern for others. So which would it be?

Had he changed at all?

Sadie looked down at what he'd written:

That's none of your business.

# *chapter thirty-four*

"Mom." Emerson shook her shoulder. "Mom, wake up."

She was asleep on the couch again with the television on, although instead of housewives, it was tuned to the news, that endless loop of tragedy and suffering.

"Mom," he said again, eyeing the sleeping pills on the coffee table with no small amount of alarm.

She sat up finally, letting the quilt slip from her shoulders and pushing her pale hair out of her face.

"Miles?" she said.

"No, Mom. It's Emerson. There's nothing new about Miles right now." He sank deep in the couch cushions beside her and hoped the breath mints he'd been sucking on would give a convincing impression of sobriety. "I just got home. I wanted to talk. Can we do that?"

"What time is it?"

"Four thirty."

"In the afternoon?"

"Yeah."

"Oh." She went to get up. "I should be getting ready for work."

He pulled her back. "No. You're not working today. Miles is missing, remember?"

She blinked. Looked confused. Then the tears came.

Emerson hugged her. He gave her tissues.

"I want to talk," he said again.

"That girl called, you know." She sniffled.

"What girl?"

"Margaret Bowman. She was pushy with me, Em."

Emerson frowned. "Why did May call *you*?"

"You left your phone. I answered it. What was I supposed to do?"

"Well, what did she want?"

"I don't know. She wants to see you. I told her you were busy, but she said she's coming over at six. Pushy, like I said."

"I want to see her, too, Mom."

She made a sound of disapproval. "You don't need to get involved with all that. Especially not right now."

*All that.* Emerson sighed. "Both her parents have Ph.D.'s, you know."

"What's your point?"

"My point is that I like her, and we're already involved. So if this is about you being bigoted or close-minded or whatever it is you always do, just drop it. God knows our family isn't anything to aspire to."

His mother burst into tears again, worse than before. Big wracking sobs shook her body.

Emerson wanted to die, right there on the spot. "Oh God, no, no, stop. I'm sorry. I didn't mean it. Don't do that. Come on. I love you. You know that."

She kept crying. Blew her nose loudly.

"I went and saw Brewster today," he said, after a moment.

She looked up. "You saw Paul?"

"Yeah."

"Why?"

"I wanted to find out more about Dad. About why he did what he did."

His mother nodded, and with her thin shoulders and wet cheeks, she looked so vulnerable, like a piece of crystal balanced on the very edge of a high shelf, that Emerson almost didn't ask his next question. He didn't want to be the one to tip her over.

But he had to.

"Mom, is it weird I don't remember you telling me Dad killed himself?"

"What are you talking about?"

"Brewster said you told me. Or that he and Uncle Petey did. But in seventh grade I heard a girl talking about it, and I swear, it was the first time I knew about it. I always thought he'd had a heart attack in his car or something. I didn't know he'd actually—"

She grabbed his arm. "I can't talk about your father right now."

Emerson paused. "Well, did you tell me or not?"

"Yes," she said. "We told you. Of course we did."

"Then why didn't I know?"

"I don't know if we should get into all this."

"We should definitely get into this. How could I forget something like that?"

"Maybe you forgot because you didn't want to remember."

"What?"

"Just what I said."

"I *forgot?*"

"It was for the best," she said. "Kids don't need to know about things like that. Poor choices and sick minds. That's grown-up stuff."

"So Dad was sick?"

"He was definitely something."

"I don't remember him being sick. I don't remember anything like that."

"That's good, Emerson. Remember him good and loving. That's what he would've wanted."

"But I don't understand. Did you *let* me forget?"

"Is that worse than not telling you the truth in the first place?"

Emerson faltered. "No. But I don't understand why you wouldn't be honest with me."

She reached out and stroked his hair. "It had nothing to do with *me,* baby. It was you. All you. You were so mad about your dad. For good reason, but your anger . . . it was scary. There was nothing I could do. So maybe sometimes I told you what you wanted to hear. That your daddy didn't choose to leave us. That his heart just gave up one night. It's almost true, if you think about it. I just wanted you to be happy. Don't you remember that?"

Emerson shook his head. What *did* he remember? He recalled flashes of his father's wake. Of wearing good shoes that were too small and getting blisters on the bottoms of his feet. Of looking at his mother's wall calendar to see his father's death date scribbled out in Sharpie, the whole thing a furious black square. He remembered returning to school a few days after the funeral and kicking a teacher in the stomach for saying he wasn't paying attention. He'd called the teacher a name, too, a really bad one, and he'd told his mom what it was when he'd gotten sent home.

"You had every reason to be furious," she'd hissed in his ear as she held him in her arms. "That woman was a real bitch to treat you like that. She deserved worse than what you did. Don't you dare let anyone tell you otherwise."

And wasn't that how it'd gone for years? Every time he was angry or acted out or got into trouble, she comforted him and let him know his feelings were valid. That's what a mother did. She took care of him even in her own pain. And when the bad stuff with Miles went down a few years later, no one was quicker to stand up for her than Emerson. She'd never hurt her kids. She loved them too much.

They were all she had.

# *chapter thirty-five*

The cellar doors lay flung open, splayed out like airplane wings. Combined with the mystery of the gravity-defying champagne bottle, as well as the champagne itself, the whole thing appeared to be some sort of strange invitation.

*Come on down, Sadie,* the doors said.

*We'll tell you our secrets.*

*We promise.*

*Just come to us.*

She crept closer. Sweat dripped down her forehead. The batten doors themselves were falling apart, on their last legs. Sadie could only see the bottoms of them, but the bare plywood that was visible was splintered and torn. Shredded, really, like someone or something had been trying very hard to get out.

Sadie stood on the edge of the cement staircase and stared into the gloomy descent. Hesitation was for cowards. Either she went down or she didn't. If some creepy serial killer was lurking around in there, waiting for the perfect moment to jump out and murder her, so be it. The way she figured, it was far more likely that whoever had cut the chain and opened the doors was up *here,* hiding in the trees or prowling among the grapevines. Because whoever it was had to be the same person who'd moved the champagne bottle and lured her in this direction. And now that someone wanted her to go into the cellar.

So she did.

She took the first step down the crumbling staircase, then the second, keeping her hand gripped tightly around the railing as she moved. The deeper she got, the better the cool air felt on her damp skin, but everything smelled stuffy, stale, and also sweet, like old fruit. She cupped her free hand over her mouth and nose.

She kept walking.

Down, down, down.

Sadie paused on the bottom step. Sunlight warmed a small patch of the dirt floor, but everything else was cloaked in blackness. The cellar stretched a good fifty feet in every direction, rows of wine barrels and shelving that ran right to the rafters, heaps of old tools and maintenance equipment that lay beneath canvas tarps, and set against the western wall was the old corking station. Sadie took a deep breath, then rose on her toes and reached for the dangling chain of the room's bare bulb socket. She pulled it.

Nothing happened.

Well, damn. The only other light source she knew of was a hand-crank lantern that was stored beneath one of the tarps. Or at least that's where it'd been the last time she'd come down here, years ago. Sadie stepped onto the dirt floor and out of the patch of sunlight.

She couldn't see anything.

She inched forward, small shuffling steps, until her feet made contact with canvas. Then she dropped to her knees and thrust one hand out, feeling all over for the lantern, ready to raise hell if anything living ran up her arm. Her fingers closed around the metal handle. She drew the lantern to her chest and turned the crank as fast as she could.

The whir of the motor filled the air and without warning, the light came on, warming the dark space with its glow.

Sadie stood up and turned around, holding the lantern out in front of her to see the rest of the space.

"Holy shit," she breathed. "Oh, Jesus."

# *chapter thirty-six*

He and May stood in the middle of his bedroom with the door closed. Emerson felt out of control. Like he was losing his mind. Like he didn't know who he was anymore.

She reached up, kissed his cheek, his forehead, the side of his neck. "What are you saying?"

"I don't know what I'm saying."

"You think your mom lied to you about your dad?"

"Shh! Keep your voice down!"

She whispered, "Is that what you think?"

"I don't know. Sort of. More, like, she let me lie to myself."

May pulled him toward her. Her hands were on his hips, gripping the belt loops of his pants. "Come on. You were just a kid, Em."

"So?"

"Kids repress bad stuff all the time. It's normal."

"It is?"

She nodded. "Your mom probably should've taken you to a therapist or something."

"Maybe. We didn't have money for things like that. We still don't."

"Oh."

Emerson felt the back of his neck go warm. "Actually, I'm pretty sure I saw a school counselor in fifth grade."

"You did?"

"Just once. She tried to talk to me about my dad, but I told her she'd be better off talking to kids who really needed her help, like those retards and idiots who can't look you in the eye without stuttering."

May's eyes went wide. "Wait. You seriously said that? Em, that's awful."

"I didn't mean it! I was *pissed*. I didn't want to talk about my feelings and cry in front of her, and I knew that's what she wanted me to do."

She softened. "Sounds like it was an emotional time."

Emerson shook his head. He never thought about it that way. Emotional. Those years were nothing but a black cloud in his mind, a swirling storm of loss and anger. But it was also a time of newfound vastness, of possibility. "Oh hell, I don't know. I mean, I *was* kind of a shitty kid back then, but we did okay, considering. Then Miles got sick and my mom had to deal with that. She got arrested, you know. Because of Trish Reed's dad."

"Your mom was arrested?"

"Yeah."

"Your mom doesn't like me."

"It's not that," he said weakly. "She just doesn't understand some things."

May pressed her lips together. "Well, why'd she get arrested?"

"The court said she was making Miles sick on purpose. It's some sort of mental thing. Munchausen syndrome by proxy. Mothers make their kids sick so they can take them to the hospital and get all this attention."

"She did that to him?"

"No! But Miles was in the hospital so much, people thought she did."

"Poor Miles," she said.

"I guess."

"Why would they think something like that if she wasn't doing it?"

"Who knows? She was always working anyway, so she couldn't have done it. That's what I told the judge, and they let her go." Emerson gave a laugh. "If anything, *I* hurt him more than she did."

"What do you mean?"

"I don't know. Once I put some window cleaner in a drink as a joke and gave it to him. He got so sick he puked blood. Had to go to the ER and everything."

May dropped her jaw. "That's *horrible*."

"Nah, he was fine. It wasn't a big deal."

"Sounds like a big deal to me. You could've killed him."

"No way. Brothers do crap like that all the time. It's guy stuff."

May didn't answer, but her hands were at her sides. She wasn't touching him anymore.

Emerson bent his knees. Wrapped both arms around her and pulled her close. "Don't think bad of me, May. Please? It was dumb. I was just a kid."

She paused. "I know."

"You're sure?"

She nodded.

"Really?"

She nodded again.

"Good," he said, smiling.

And then he kissed her.

## *chapter thirty-seven*

Birds. The birds were everywhere.

Dozens of them.

They were spread out on the dirt. Across the marble-topped slab. They were nailed to the wall and the wood beams that ran up to the rafters. All with their wings pulled wide as if in flight. All with their heads missing.

Sadie walked around slowly, taking stock of it all. There were hawks, crows, pigeons, robins, sparrows, tiny hummingbirds with green iridescent feathers, and one grotesque creature that took Sadie a moment to recognize as a wild turkey, maybe even the old tom she'd seen strutting around in the road the other day. Its dark body was positioned awkwardly beside the others, as if in death, the wretched thing believed it might finally soar with its lighter-weight counterparts.

In addition to the birds, there were words written everywhere, splashed across the walls in bright dripping letters that Sadie mistook for blood before realizing it was paint. Someone had used an old brush and red paint as bright as a berry.

The words read:

*salute*
*press*
*perry*
*passé*
*riposte*
*thrust*
*touché*

And beneath that:

*help me*
*please*
*help*

# *chapter thirty-eight*

Emerson pulled back from the kiss with May. Not that the kissing wasn't making him feel good on a day when nothing felt good, but his limbs, his whole being felt restless, unsatisfied. He walked away from her and over to the window where he stared out at the street below. There was a boy jogging with a large dog, some kind of shepherd mix, and two kids wrapped in beach towels walking home from the river. They both wore flip-flops. "You know, I realized, this thing with Miles, it's happened before."

"What's happened?" May asked from the other side of the room.

"Him disappearing."

"It *has*?"

Emerson nodded, still gazing out the window. "Yup. When he was seven. He disappeared for a whole day. Freaked everyone the hell out."

"Where was he? How'd you find him?"

"The owner of this vineyard where my mom used to work found him. He'd gotten locked down in this old cellar on the back of their property and couldn't get out."

"Scary."

"The vineyard guy was so mad. Like, really pissed. He fired my mom the next week. Said Miles could've died down there."

"Well, that's kind of crappy. I mean, it was an accident, right?"

He turned to look at her. May was sitting on his bed, long legs folded beneath her like a fawn. "Miles was different after that, you know? Just weird. Kind of a weird kid. He had nightmares. Got picked on in school. Started getting sick all the time. I should've felt bad for him, but sometimes . . ."

"Sometimes what?"

Emerson shook his head. "I don't know how to explain it. Sometimes it's hard to feel bad for someone who's always suffering."

"You think?" May sounded doubtful.

"I don't know," he said again, closing his eyes and rubbing his fingers in small circles against the lids. "Maybe that's just me."

# chapter thirty-nine

Sadie's heart sank. She knew who'd written these words. Without a doubt.

*Miles the fencer.*

He was the boy from the cellar, wasn't he? The one her dad had rescued like a hero, all those years ago. The details were faint in her mind, soft wisps of remembrance. Sadie hadn't been there when it'd happened, but she'd heard about it, heard the words her father had muttered in Mandarin as he chained the doors shut for good. At the time it made her wonder if he'd seen the things she and Emerson had stockpiled down there, and if he had, what he thought of her. But her father never said anything about that.

Which was infinitely worse than if he had.

What he *did* tell her was that a small boy had gotten locked in the cellar. Some sort of accident or misunderstanding. However it had happened, the child had spent hours in there, alone and unable to escape. Sadie couldn't be bothered to care much about some random boy, or even a nonrandom one, but even she knew whatever that child endured was the stuff of nightmares. Trapped amidst death and reek and rotting things. He must've been frantic. Traumatized.

And now, years later, for some reason, he'd returned.

*Why?*

Sadie went to one of the painted walls. Pressed her fingers against the words. They were sticky, all of them. Her fingers came back red.

Minutes stretched, and the lantern's glow began to fade. On legs that felt weak but no longer drunk, Sadie walked back to the staircase and stared up toward the cellar entrance.

At that bright patch of sunlight.

At that blue, blue sky.

*Disturbed,* he'd told her in her car the last time she'd given him a ride. *I'm a disturbed person.*

"Miles," she whispered into the void. "Come on, kid. Show me where the hell you are. Let me fucking help."

# *chapter forty*

The girl was calling his name.

That meant she'd found his message. To her. To the world.

She called out for him again, louder this time, and Miles whimpered from where he lay hidden in the bushes and shadows behind the old press. Like a weak spot worn bare by wanting, some thin part of him stretched and ached to go to her. To spread his wings. To share his pain and be heard. She'd done that before. She'd listened to him, without judgment or appeasement, without wanting to fix him. But he didn't go. His wings were long clipped, his soul long scarred, and what he'd left in that bunker for her to find—those birds that couldn't fly; those words he couldn't say—was the very best he could do.

The future, *his* future, was almost here. He couldn't deny that.

*Duty to harm,* the wind whispered.

*You know what you have to do, boy.*

Miles squeezed his eyes shut.

He clapped his hands over his ears.

He slipped into the past from which he'd come, but would never understand.

Their family was a happy family. Then their father died, and his brother became angry and their mother became sad.

No.

That wasn't how the story went.

His brother was angry and their mother was distant, and their father was sick. Their father tried to get help for his sickness, but the help he found didn't work. It only made him sicker. And sadder.

Then their father died.

And Miles grew scared.

There was no one left to guard him.

When Miles was small, he watched his brother Emerson all the time. He watched him the way a mouse would watch a sleeping cat. When their mother started a new job taking care of a sick, old man out at a fancy winery, Miles did his best to watch from her side or behind her apron strings. The apron strings were metaphorical, of course, because their mother was a nurse, not a housewife or a cook. She took care of people who were dying, and some days, when Emerson was at his cruelest, Miles wished he'd die, too.

Those sprawling acres brought something dark out of his brother.

Not that he'd ever been funny or warm or protective or any of those things brothers were shown to be in books or movies. But the days spent running through the grapevines, heady with sun and abandon, harvested a new side of Emerson. A savagery.

Or maybe that side of him had always been there. Maybe he'd slipped from the womb with his cold eyes and quick temper. With his compulsive need to do anything he could get away with and take what he wanted. Maybe it was just that without their father's guidance, there was no one left to curb his urges—no one to worry his soul or snap him back in line and teach him that strength could be a weakness sometimes, the very, very worst kind of weakness. Their mother wasn't up to the task, that was for sure. She was too lost in her denial. Her avoidance. Grief was one thing, and it was understandable, but Miles couldn't help but wonder if his father had ever felt the same scraping emptiness when he tried to talk to her about things that mattered. As if her heart were a lock to which he had no key.

As if he would always, always be alone.

In that open season of bruises and seeping wounds and down-the-stairs shoving, Emerson wasn't the only one Miles had to watch out for. There was a girl at the winery, too. She never touched him, not once, but she was brash and loud and talked back to adults without an ounce of fear. Worst of all, she liked Emerson, and that meant Miles knew well enough to stay out of her way.

There were times his mother wouldn't let him stay with her. This usually happened when the old man needed certain things done, like his sponge bath or pain meds or had to go to the bathroom. Sometimes it happened when she was simply sick and tired of having him around.

"Scoot," she'd say. "Go on. You're not a baby. Someday you're going to have to take care of me, you know. So you'd better learn to be brave. To stick up for yourself. Like your brother does."

Those were the times when Miles roamed the big house alone, quiet as the smallest beast. He absorbed the secrets he saw and heard because no one knew he was there.

He learned that the lady of the house wasn't happy. Her daddy was dying and Miles knew about that sort of sadness, about the way it could eat you up with an ache that went on and on, flowing like the tides, both high and low, but never ending, never letting go. *Daddylost,* he'd come to call it inside his head, and even though she was an adult, the lady sounded like a child when she cried. Miles knew he sounded like a child when he cried, too, but he *was* a child, no matter what his mother said.

Once Miles went to the lady when she was all alone and spilling over with her daddylost pain. He went to her because no one else did, not even her husband, who heard her, but just closed his office door and hid behind the beauty of old guns and old books and turned up the opera music he was listening to in there.

She lay sprawled on a fancy couch in a special porch room that was part inside and part outside and opened onto a huge garden. The room smelled wonderful like lilacs and night jasmine and tea with honey, but the lady was crying so hard that nothing about it felt good. Miles's nerves rattled into rickety little freight trains threatening to go off their rails. He didn't know what to do or how to make her feel better, so he'd just gone to her and stroked her back. Her skin was warm. Hot, even, like bread fresh from the oven. She fell asleep while he touched her and started to snore.

Miles also learned that the man of the house longed not to be there. He had a pattern of coming and going. Of turning toward and turning away. His daughter noticed most when he was gone. His wife, too. It made them both sad and angry. Pretty soon Miles realized that the man didn't understand his wife or daughter. He tried to, but they confused him. He didn't like confusion.

Soon, he didn't like them.

On occasion Miles let his guard down. That was always a mistake. Like the time he let Emerson and the girl feed him lunch. It didn't make sense that his brother would do something nice for him, but when he started getting sick on the ride home, he'd understood. His mother told the hospital that he must have gotten into some cleaning products when she wasn't looking. And even though they both knew she was lying, Miles didn't say differently because he liked the peace of the hospital and how the people there were nice and he didn't have to keep up his endless vigilance with avoiding his brother. That little bit of peace made up for how bad he felt, and when he was older he learned to chase that hospital room peace. Through pills. Through microbes. Through self-induced harm.

After the poisoned-drink incident, Miles followed Emerson and the girl a few times, wondering if there was a way he could get back at them. Getting back wasn't a concept he liked, but he liked survival and not being hurt, so he considered it. He watched the two of them go in and out of some hidden bunker that was built into the ground out by the boggy creek.

*Dorothy doors* were how he thought of the entrance to their hideout, because the twin batten doors reminded him of the one that led to the storm cellar in *The Wizard of Oz.* Miles longed to know what was down there and if he could use their secrets to protect himself, and when they were gone one day because the girl was visiting relatives and Emerson was down by the highway shooting squirrels with a slingshot, Miles snuck in.

And his nightmares came alive.

*The birds. Oh god. Here they were.*

For months his dreams had been haunted by images of dead birds trying to fly, crows mostly, and Miles hadn't understood why this was. But now, down in this horrible bunker, he was surrounded by bird corpses—the exact images of his dreams. There was a whole pile of them, thrown carelessly onto the floor: their tiny bodies mutilated, many with missing heads and claws and wings. A soft sob of horror escaped Miles as he stared at them all.

His dreams hadn't prepared him for this. He loved animals. They had kind eyes, and when they touched you there was never pain. Or fear. But the birds. The *birds.* It broke his heart to see them.

It was just *so sad.*

Miles started to cry.

That's when the sound of shattering glass filled the bunker. Miles jumped, and the Dorothy doors above him slammed shut with a resounding thud.

His whole world went black.

Miles stood, trembling, every hair on his body risen in fear. He listened to the soft clunk and clang of the metal chain being wrapped methodically through the door handles. He heard Emerson's soft teasing laugh. He bolted up the staircase, his shoes crunching on shards of the broken lightbulb, and pounded on the bottom of the doors to be let out. He screamed. He yelled. He threw himself at the doors and clawed wood until his fingers bled. But nothing happened.

He was trapped.

In the dark.

Alone.

He screamed more. Fought more. All useless. Eventually his voice went hoarse. Eventually his tears dried up. Eventually he curled on the top step by the locked doors and slept.

Time passed strangely after that, a tumbling roll of being that ceased to make sense. He was more than daddylost. He was utterly lost in every sense of the word. He couldn't tell day from night. Sleep from wakefulness.

Life from death.

Sometime later, Miles became aware that the birds were talking to him. From the black depths of the bunker they whispered and chattered their truth to him. They used their minds, their broken fluttering wings, to communicate, to ease his fear. They understood that his wings were broken, too. Finally he slunk back down the stairs where he sat on the dirt floor, gathered them all into his lap, and picked them up, one by one.

Like seashells, he held each ruined bird to his ear and listened to what it had to say. His dreams hadn't been dreams at all, they told him, but pieces of a moment yet to come. A moment only he could see. A power only he could wield.

After he was done listening, Miles tossed them each into the air.

Here was the future, he thought. Here is my gift. Right in my most powerless hands.

*Yes! Yes!* The birds crowed as they flew.

*The future was truth!*

*The future was his!*

And death, like the dark horror who called himself his brother, was inescapable.

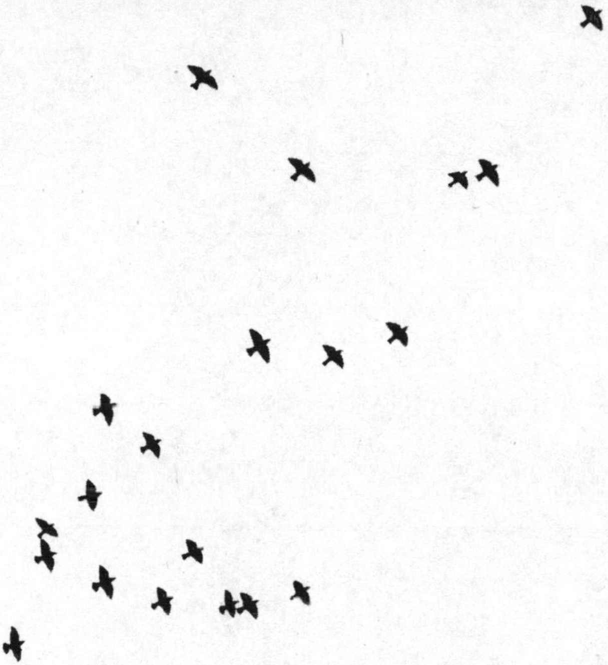

# *part 4*

## Delicate Monsters

The things that we love tell us what we are.

—St. Thomas Aquinas

# chapter forty-one

Monday morning came, bleak and solemn, and Emerson tried going to school. Miles was still missing and still presumed dead, but he craved routine. He craved normalcy. He craved not being trapped in his apartment with his miserable mother, having to grieve and watch the minutes tick by while nothing happened.

But when he got to campus, it was all too much—the stimulation. The crowds. The hive-mind hum. Emerson's hands shook and his lungs burned. He didn't know what else to do, so he sat and took a few shots from a newly acquired bottle of Wild Turkey—this one slipped into the waistband of his jeans in the middle of the night at the grocery store—before getting out of the Mustang and stumbling toward the main quad. It was 7:45 a.m.

Trey saw him first, which was a relief. Winding through the bustling courtyard before the first-period bell, he reached an arm out and slapped Emerson on the shoulder. His eyes were red, like he'd been crying. A jarring sight. As long as Emerson had known Trey, he'd only seen him cry once, and that was when Dahlia Temple dumped him in the ninth grade after promising him they could go all the way.

"You all right?" he asked Emerson. "I wanted to call over the weekend, but I didn't know . . . Giovanna said I shouldn't bother you, but . . ."

Emerson gave a boozy smile. "It's fine. Really. And let's not talk about it here, all right?"

"Sure."

"I've been drinking," he admitted.

"Okay."

"Now I kind of want to get shit-faced."

"Good for you."

"You want to join me?"

Trey looked around and nodded. "Hell, yeah."

"I fucked up," Emerson said when they were in his car together out by the country club golf course. He'd parked on the edge of the frontage road, backed up against a sound wall, and he was sitting behind the wheel with the bottle of Wild Turkey clutched between his legs. Trey lay sprawled in the backseat with his feet up, smoking a joint. He held it out to Emerson, who shook his head. "Coach tests you, you're dead."

Trey waved a hand and took another drag. "He won't test during preseason."

"He's cracking down this year."

"Whatever. I don't care. No school's going to pick me up anyway. I'd rather play at the goddamn Y then bust my ass for another five hundred season."

"You don't mean that."

"Hell if I don't." Trey lifted his chin. "So how'd you fuck up?"

Emerson reached out and flipped the radio on. Classic rock. An old Metallica song was playing. The one about praying to God and laying down to sleep.

"A lot of ways," he said.

"You can't feel guilty about this kind of thing, man. You can't. It'll eat you up. Those assholes who hurt Miles, they're the one with blood on their hands."

Emerson must have looked as queasy as he felt, because Trey quickly added, "Shit. I'm sorry. I meant that as a metaphor or an allegory or whatever. He's gonna show up. He's gonna be fine. I know he is."

"I don't know. I don't know that I believe that anymore."

"I do."

"I hurt him once, Trey."

"How?"

"I locked him in this cellar when we were kids. On purpose. Told my mom he was out playing, and I left him there for hours. A whole day. I never went back."

Trey choked on his joint and started coughing. "Shut up. That's nothing. That has nothing to do with anything."

Didn't it, though? Emerson sighed. "Sadie Su's dad was the one who found him. He was *furious*. Fired my mom the next week. Said I was a bad influence on his daughter."

"Yeah, right. Sadie's a bitch all on her own."

"I know."

"She really is."

"Miles was crazy, man," Emerson said sadly. "I mean, he was really, really crazy."

"Nah."

"He was. He told me he saw visions. Did you know that? He thought he knew when people were going to die."

*"Fuck,"* Trey said, and Emerson realized suddenly that *he* was crying. His shoulders shuddered and his throat stung, and tears ran down his face, his lips, into his mouth. For the first time since his brother had vanished, he was crying because he knew in his heart Miles wouldn't be coming home. Because he knew in his heart that *he* was the reason his brother had left in the first place. Because he knew that if by some miracle of fate Miles ever did return, it wouldn't be to kill himself. It would probably be to kill *him*.

Rightly so.

Emerson swiped his arm beneath his nose. "I made him sick once, too."

"Come on," Trey said. "Don't."

"More than once, really. All those times he went to the hospital, I think it was because of me. Not literally. Like, *I* didn't actually make him sick every time, but I think he did it to himself to get away from me. Sometimes he'd get physically ill just from me talking to him. He'd start gagging or his stomach would act up, and I don't know, it made me *more* mad when he'd do that. That's fucked, isn't it? It's really fucked."

"Don't do this. It's not your fault."

"But it *is.* I used to yell at him, Trey. Hit him. Shove him. Tell him when he did stupid shit, which was always. Probably other things I can't even remember. Told myself it wasn't a big deal at the time. But I think I knew. I always knew."

"You're his brother. Your dad was gone. You had to do that shit, man. My dad does worse to me now. He's an asshole."

Emerson sighed. "I found this notebook of his yesterday. He used it for drawing, I guess. It was hidden in this drawer in our bathroom. You know what else was in there?"

Trey shook his head. "Mmmm, tell me there was at least one naked chick in that notebook. With, like, really big titties."

"No titties."

"Dicks?"

"No dicks, either. There was nothing like that. But under the notebook Miles had all these pills, not just bottles, but whole *boxes* of them, and there were old syringes and plastic containers filled with some kind of mold. I don't even know where he would get that kind of stuff. But he might've been using it for years. He might've been, I don't know, really screwing himself up. Because of me."

Trey sat up. Stared at him with sleepy eyes. "Are you saying Miles was doing drugs?"

*"No,"* Emerson said. "That's not what I'm saying at all."

"Then what?"

"Fuck. Never mind. I'm too fucked up."

They sat in silence again, Trey still smoking and staring at the roof of the car. Emerson still drinking himself into oblivion. His head was spinning already, round and round, a slow sickly loop of regret.

Miles.

May.

Sadie.

The cat.

"Trey?" he said.

"Huh?"

"You ever do something bad? Something you regretted but couldn't take back?"

"What kind of bad?"

"Really bad."

Trey was quiet for a moment. Then: "Yeah."

"What did you do about it? How did you deal with, you know, the guilt?"

Trey made a fist. Ghost-punched the air in front of him. "What the hell do you think I did? I fucking said I was sorry."

# *chapter forty-two*

Sadie was frustrated by everything and everyone at the moment. This included stupid Roman Bender, because the last time she'd heard from him, he'd told her that she should know where to find Dumpster Boy.

Only she didn't know.

Not even after going down into that cellar and seeing what Miles had done and the kind of help he so clearly needed.

Not even after spending the whole weekend searching for the kid—scouring the far corners of the vineyard, driving through town, looking everywhere.

This not knowing bothered Sadie. It pricked her worse than sand in her bed or a zit on her ass, and it was the reason she chose to spend most of her Monday lingering around the school office, eavesdropping and hoping to learn something new. Her efforts paid off; she was able to find out that the boys who'd beaten up Miles had come forward to the police that morning. From what she could gather, they were sophomores, a pair of them. Both lacrosse players, both known for their thuggish, entitled ways—destined, no doubt, for years of Ivy League grandeur, hopefully highlighted by episodes of binge drinking and subsequent contraction of the herpes virus.

No one, however, seemed to think the two boys had anything to do with Miles's vanishing. Sadie didn't think so, either, but she still couldn't help but wonder if they knew what it felt like to be hurt. And frightened. And terrorized. Like Charlie Burns, she had a feeling they didn't. She had a feeling that once someone was seen as a victim, it was hard for people to see them as anything else. It made sense the same would hold true for the victimizer.

But maybe she'd always known that.

Dr. CMT caught her hanging around after lunch and mistook her presence for something it wasn't.

"You're early, Sadie," he said. "I'm afraid our appointment isn't until three."

"Fuck off," Sadie snapped.

"Excuse me?"

"I know what you did. You've been talking to the cops about Miles. Telling them things he told you in private, making them think he hurt himself. Some therapist you are. You can't even keep your dumb mouth shut."

"Now, wait a minute." His cheeks went pink. "I can assure you I didn't do anything that wasn't required of me by law."

Sadie snorted. "Oh, please. I saw you on the news. Talking to that lady reporter about how *concerned* you are. Acting like your cock spun gold. You love the attention. Don't pretend you don't."

"Maybe we should talk about this in private."

"Maybe we shouldn't. I'm not talking to you about anything. You're an asshole. A lying rat bastard asshole."

"Sadie—"

"Leave me alone!" she screamed, and everyone turned to stare. Dr. CMT, whose cheeks had gone even pinker, just dipped his head, raised his hands, and backed away, retreating to his scummy prison cell of an office.

When he was gone, Sadie set her jaw and ignored the staring. She turned on her heel, then walked straight out of the building. She already had plans to drive out to Petaluma to see Wilderness Camp Chad after school, but she yanked her phone out and texted him that she was coming over now.

Sadie didn't care if she got kicked out for ditching class.

She didn't care if he did, either.

The drive wasn't far. Petaluma was an agricultural town that sat to the west of the wine country, closer to the ocean. At some point in time, it had dubbed itself "Egg Capital of the World!" which was about all anyone needed to know about that. Chad's family owned a farm out there. They had a red barn and everything, complete with egg-laying chickens, goats, and even a small donkey. It was disgustingly wholesome. When Sadie got there, she and Chad took their clothes off in the second-floor hayloft to fool around in the god-awful autumn heat.

She inspected his naked body. Not the part he wanted her to, but his wrists. Those pink lightning-streak scars.

"I don't like you," she told him, lying back in the straw.

"I know that," he said.

"I'm serious. I don't like one damn thing about you."

"Girl, don't be mean." He nuzzled her tits and kissed her bare stomach. Moved his mouth lower. And lower. "Can't you just enjoy this one thing without being mean?"

# *chapter forty-three*

"Emerson," May whispered. "Why don't you ever let me?"

It was late Monday afternoon, day scraping against evening, and the two of them lay together on her bed again, their bodies tangled in the sheets. It was almost like a do-over of a week ago, when everything was normal and this whole thing with Miles had never happened. Emerson had sobered up since the morning, for the most part, and like the last time they'd been here, he'd made her shiver and gasp with his hands. But also like last time, he wouldn't let her touch him.

It still felt wrong.

It felt wrong, he realized through a sick throbbing in his head, because things *weren't* totally normal a week ago. They'd just been a different kind of bad. Secret bad.

"It's not you," he whispered back, pushing her hand away, although he could still see the hurt in her eyes.

"Is it Miles?" she asked.

"*No.* You make me feel better about that. God, when I'm with you, it's the only time I feel better. I swear, May. Without you, I'd be lost. I'd be insane."

"Then what is it?"

"I don't know. Maybe . . . I'm just really sensitive?" Emerson felt his cheeks burn with the lie, but he'd read about it online. Some guys really were sensitive down there. So much so, it was painful to have anyone else touch them. It took this whole process of gradual habituation for them to be able to enjoy sex. Emerson thought if he could convince May that this was his problem, then he could focus on making her feel good.

And maybe his guilt would go away.

Finally.

May perked up at this response, this acquittal of her blame. "Sensitive. Like it hurts?"

"Yeah."

"So does that mean you can't—"

"No, well, I *can*. But only by myself."

"Oh," she said brightly. "Then show me."

"What?"

A sly grin crept across May's lips. "I want to see you do it."

Emerson's heart raced with panic, but how could he do anything other than what she was asking? He couldn't hurt her more than he already had. He couldn't make her feel like *she* was the problem.

So he sat up.

He pulled his boxers down.

The air felt cool against his skin, and Emerson's mind tingled with a strong sense of *rightness*. Maybe this was it, then. Maybe this was his moment of absolution. After all, this is what started the whole thing in the first place: a brief act that any guy, anywhere, did countless times, over and over, without care, without consequence. An act that seemed small if you squinted at it just right, but that had become big enough to swallow him whole.

So he would do it now. For her.

And it would be okay.

Or not.

"What's wrong?" she asked after a few moments of her watching and him failing, and that's when Emerson realized there *was* care behind his actions. Intent, too. There always had been. It was just a truth he hadn't been willing to see. A desire he hadn't been willing to want. But what Emerson was willing to see or want wasn't the point. Behavior was what mattered.

The mind would follow.

Emerson looked at May. Beautiful May, with her delicate turn of her ankle.

With her ice slowly melting.

"Close your eyes," he said gruffly.

"What?"

"Close them. And lay on the floor. Play dead."

"Em—"

"Play like you're dead."

May stared at him, and she wasn't frightened or upset or offended. Her eyes were full of wonder and trust and everything good he didn't deserve.

She got up and lay on the floor for him. She closed her eyes.

She played dead.

Then there. *There.* That was what he needed.

The rush.

The reverence.

Every damn bit of it.

But who was he in that moment? Tingling and rare, Emerson didn't know. Didn't need to know. Like that night at the party, up in the bathroom, he was just so *present*. He was so much. He was high, then low. He was naked and nerves, fever and bliss. Then he was every molecule sparkling and reaching, reaching, reaching for a goal so dazzling and perfect, it almost didn't matter that when it was over, when his heart pitched back down from the heavens, he found that the blackness was right there inside of him again. As if it had never left.

Because it hadn't.

And then Emerson *did* know.

He knew the lies he'd been telling himself.

He knew what he had to do.

So he went to May, and he told her.

*Everything.*

# *chapter forty-four*

The next morning, Sadie thought she actually caught a glimpse of Dumpster Boy on her way to school. She drove past the coffee shop and the Motel 6, and she could've sworn she saw him there, crouched behind that nasty 7-11 Dumpster. Sadie swung a hasty U-turn—illegal, of course—but by the time she circled around and pulled into the lot, the place was deserted. There was no one.

Nothing.

After that, she got to fencing class early, quickly changing clothes and showing up first in the gym. But he wasn't there, either, and it was clear no one expected him to be. Sadie stood alone, arms folded, and glowered at each of the faces surrounding her, those flat expressions of laziness and disinterest. She wondered if any of them actually knew the missing boy had been in their class, or if they were all too dumb and self-absorbed. The PE teacher didn't even say anything. He just stood there, rubbing his bleary eyes, and pointed for Sadie to partner up with a senior girl.

It was as if Miles had never existed.

A gray cloud hovered over Sadie the rest of the morning. She didn't feel like herself, which she hated, but in feeling that way, she recalled a gloomy piece of advice her father had given her in their Finland hotel room, back in February, the very last time they'd been together.

"The most dangerous lie in America isn't a political one," he'd told her, as he stood by the plate glass window, gazing down at the frigid Helsinki skyline. "It's the lie that who we are is some fixed self-determined truth. That there's some absolute *us*-ness in our character that's unchangeable and real, and that we have an obligation to be true to this us-ness, no matter the cost. As if who we are could exist in the absence of other people. We're no more eternal than a single star, Sadie. Remember that. We shine. We burn out. But together, we can light the sky."

"Well, I'm not all that American," Sadie had replied, because she'd lived abroad. She'd traveled the world.

But whether her father agreed with her assessment or not, she didn't know, because unlike that afternoon in the kitchen when she was a little girl and he'd begged her not to be so cruel, he didn't bother answering her. He'd simply settled in the chair by the window and closed his eyes.

He'd gone to sleep.

Sadie's gray cloud grew darker. By the time third period rolled around, she was in no mood to see Emerson Tate and his mopey grief and guilty glare. So instead of going to her Research Methods class,

Sadie snuck up onto the school's roof to smoke. While she was there, she wrote to Roman for what would be the second-to-last time:

---

What did you do after?

---

She knew she didn't need to explain more than that. *After* meant after she'd hurt him. After the months she'd spent pushing him away and putting him down. After he'd kept coming back, no matter what she did or how horribly she treated him. After she decided to confront him, and finally ask what it was he saw in her, why he still wanted to be her friend.

"I don't like myself," he told her. "And you don't like me, either. That has to mean something. I know it does."

And wasn't that him giving her permission to hurt him? It felt as if he were handing over the reins of his own suicidal impulses. That was how Sadie understood it. Of course, it was how she wanted to understand it, because for her, toying with him and offering him hope every now and then that she might actually find value in him as a human being, before pulling it all out from under him, was pure pleasure. It was everything and more. So there'd been no reason *why* she'd done what she'd done.

There'd just been no reason not to.

So *after* meant after the dark January evening when she'd blindfolded Roman and driven him into the woods in the middle of a New York winter with only his Kentucky-weight jacket and left him alone with a map and a series of instructions. Instructions that would lead him to a secret party, she told him, part of an ancient Rothshire tradition. The lies had rolled off her tongue with grease-slicked ease. Only there was snow in the forecast that night, an icy blizzard, and the map she left led him far from any signs of life, ensuring that he ended up on the bank of a frozen river with the wind whipping, while the thermometer hovered close to the zero mark. He was out there all night until a helicopter spotted him the following morning. Disoriented and near death, he'd told the cops it had just been a prank. Never mind that Sadie wasn't even the one who'd gone looking for him or called the police; that had been the school when they realized he'd missed curfew. Still, Roman insisted, it was a joke between friends.

Nothing more.

After, Sadie had been brought up on criminal charges, but without his testimony against her, she got off with probation, expulsion from school, and an agreement for her mother to send her to the therapeutic wilderness camp. And after, Roman, who suffered serious medical complications as well as a severe mental breakdown, had gone home to his family and, as far as she knew, hadn't left his house to go outside in over eight months. Not once.

It took a while for him to reply. But he finally did.

---

That's the thing about after, Sadie. It's still happening, and there's no one answer to what you want to know. I'm living after. Every second. Every minute. Every day. But I'm living, and there's that. So here are a few of my immediate afters. Moments I'm not proud of:

After . . .

I wanted to die.

I wanted to kill myself.

I wanted to kill you.

Clearly, I didn't do any of those things, although I can see how for someone else, it would be easy to get stuck in one of those afters and not let go. But I moved on, because that's who I am. I realize this now, and I'm starting to be okay with it. For one, I'm a pacifist. I'm also afraid of death. But more than anything, what keeps me here on this earth and lets me live with my failures is the knowledge that I am a lamb among wolves.

I am not you.

---

Sadie clenched her jaw. She wrote back:

---

I did it to make you not want me. I did it to make you leave me the fuck alone.

---

He didn't respond. Sadie puffed harder on her cigarette and stared down into the narrow courtyard. Her heart stopped.

There, alone in the shadows beneath her, stood Dumpster Boy. She recognized his thin body and the way he hunched his back and his floppy blond hair that hung in his eyes and reached past the collar of his shirt. She couldn't believe he was actually here, but he was real, definitely real, and her instinct was to lean over and call to him with a lazy "hey, asshole" or something to let him know where she was, but in a way that didn't tell him how thrilled she was to see him. And she was, wasn't she?

*Thrilled.*

But Sadie stopped mid-lean. Miles had something gripped in his hands, an object long and dark. A gun, she realized with quick-rising horror. He's got a goddamn gun. Then something cold and awful wriggled through her, because when Sadie thought about the broken birds and the words he'd left in the abandoned cellar, and how close to her house he must have been hiding, all this time, it was clear he'd stolen one of her father's rifles. Right off the wall from his prized gun collection that he kept unlocked in his study. Of course Miles would know the guns were there. Of course Miles had seen them before.

*riposte*

*thrust*

*touché*

Miles the fencer, planning his attack.

All this time.

Of *course.*

Sadie threw her cigarette on the ground and glanced at her phone.

Five minutes until the bell rang and the courtyard would be flooded. Her own Research Methods class would walk right into his line of fire.

"No," she muttered. "No, no, no."

Sadie ran as fast as she could, but she wasn't fast enough. The bell went off just as her foot slammed down on the first floor of the main building. Students crowded into the hall, but she shouted and pushed and shoved people out of the way, then kicked open the door that led into the courtyard.

Miles stood by the wall near a narrow strip of grass and an untended butterfly garden. His back was to her and somehow the saddest thing wasn't the way the oversized vintage rifle dwarfed his childlike hands or the cord of tension that streaked between his shoulder blades. It was the fact that he was wearing the same goddamn clothes he'd been wearing the last time she'd seen him. He'd sat in her car in that same dopey T-shirt with the picture of a fish on the back. It was also the day he'd told her he could see the future.

Was this what he'd seen?

Sadie bit back a cry. She didn't know. It didn't matter. The rifle was on his shoulder now. His finger on the trigger. He was scanning the crowd, looking for someone.

*Who?*

She sprinted hard. Launched at him from behind, knocking them both to the ground while she grabbed for the gun. He came back at her, swinging wildly. They grappled and rolled.

"Stop it," she barked. "It's me, motherfucker! Me! I'm trying to help you. Like you asked me to! You can't do this. You *can't.* They'll kill you. Don't you get that?"

But no, Miles didn't get it, and no, he didn't stop. He fought

Sadie like a treed cat, all fear and claws and fanged desperation. Soon people around them were screaming. About the gun. About her. About *him*. They realized who he was—the missing boy, the one they'd never cared about. But they cared now, because he was back from the dead.

Sadie reached for Miles again, but he shoved her with the butt of the rifle, slamming her head off the grass and snapping her jaw. Ears ringing, Sadie rolled to her right and scrambled forward into the butterfly garden. Wood chips scraped her hands, her knees, tangled in her hair, but her elbow bumped against something hard—a stake, a metal garden stake, the kind used to hold plants too weak to hold themselves. Sadie yanked it from the dirt. The stake was surprisingly heavy. She nearly dropped it. Held on. Had just gotten a good grip when Miles lunged for her. He grabbed her wrist. And twisted.

The pain was bright and shattering. Sadie writhed like a rattler, bucking this way and that. Finally wrenching free, she lashed out with the stake, thrusting as hard as she could until the sharpened tip made contact. It struck his cheek and sank deep.

Like a nightmare, blood exploded, spraying everywhere, onto the ground, on her. Miles cried out, the horrible anguish of a hurt boy, and grabbed for his face. There were tears in his eyes. The rifle tumbled to the ground.

Sadie picked it up and ran.

There was more screaming, more crowds, more people scattering in every direction. Sadie saw kids and teachers alike dropping to the ground, ducking for cover. And she heard voices shrieking at her to *stop*!

To *put it the hell down*!

To *give herself up before she got hurt*!

Oh shit. Shit. Shit. Shit. They thought the gun was hers. They thought Miles had been trying to wrestle it away from her. That's what it looked like. There was blood all over her. *His* blood. Maybe they even thought she'd abducted him or something horrible, and now, like some God-given miracle, he was finally free.

Sadie ran faster. Fine. Good. Whatever. Let those fuckers think that. Let them believe in her badness and not in his. It was the truth, after all. She headed for her car on pure adrenaline instinct. Once there, she heaved the rifle onto the passenger's seat and slid behind the wheel. She started the engine. Threw the car in reverse. The tires squealed and left black marks. She gunned it out of there.

What the hell else was she going to do?

# *chapter forty-five*

*Was it possible to fall so far from greatness?*

*Was this, then, his destiny?*

Emerson woke late Tuesday morning. He swung his feet to the floor and looked at the clock. It was ten thirty. That meant he was missing Research Methods, which was fine by him. He hadn't set his alarm on purpose, because he didn't plan on going to school today. In fact, the dreams Emerson had been having of late meant he didn't plan on doing anything anyone might expect from him.

What he did do, however, was take a long shower, his mind filling with steam as the hot spray peppered his body like sniper fire.

After, he dressed in clean clothes taken from the laundry and kissed his still-sleeping mother on the cheek. Then he got into his dead father's '64 dynasty green Mustang and drove it out toward the highway.

He felt the sun on his face.

He felt the breeze in his hair.

He felt so very, very guilty.

Despite the guilt, or maybe because of it, Emerson kept driving, kept picking up speed. He absorbed the thrum of the engine and bump-press-roll of the pavement beneath his tires. A song came on the radio that made him feel sad, but in his sadness he also found a rich sense of satisfaction, one that ran both deep and profound.

This, he thought, this was the way a good-bye should be for someone like him.

Solitary.

Secretive.

Shameful.

Maybe a little bit liberating, too.

And it really was a good-bye. A cowardly one, sure, seeing as he was running with his tail between his legs, unwilling to answer for the things he'd done and the pain he'd caused. But the way Emerson saw it was like this: his family, his friends, they deserved better than him. Only better wasn't something he was willing or able to give. It never had been.

It never would be.

So he wouldn't be back. Not to Sonoma or the apartment. Not ever. He'd known that yesterday when he'd been with May. He'd known even before her eyes turned cold and hard, and she asked him to leave before she called the goddamn police and told them what he'd done.

But maybe he'd always known. Maybe the cool winds of fate and the flag-snap flutter of destiny had always been there, tickling his spine, whispering in his ear *it's gonna catch up with you boy one of these days the truth'll come back so you'd better go go go,* until finally, Emerson couldn't help but listen. There was only so much ruin the mind could rationalize. There was only so much badness that could be suppressed for so long. His guilt, on its own, was utterly meaningless—just a showy type of magic that changed nothing because changing nothing was the endgame all along. Words like *absolution* and *forgiveness* and *redemption* would never apply to someone like him. Those terms were just abstractions.

Names for what other people called the moments between darkness.

In the end it was simple: May was a good person. He was not. The way he'd fallen for her that day at the poolside party when she'd played badminton in the sun and he'd watched her breasts move and her brown skin glisten, that wasn't love. That was desperation, a sad last gasp at something he would never find.

Like Miles, Emerson could see the future, too.

Like Miles, it both awed and frightened him.

The Mustang raced out of town.

He never once looked back.

# *chapter forty-six*

*Oh, Miles, you dumb kid. You told me.*

*I should've known.*

Sadie squeezed her eyes shut, then opened them again. Everything in her field of vision was shimmery and distant, the landscape whipping by in a hot blur. This moment was too surreal not to be real. City cops were riding right on her ass, a long train of them. The Doppler wail of their sirens filled her car and rattled her mind.

But she kept going. And going. She had no other choice. After peeling out of the school lot, she'd just about reached the main road when the first patrol car came up from behind, lights flashing, voice on the loudspeaker shouting at her to pull over. Should she have stopped then? Probably. Was it too late now? Definitely. Instead she'd hit the gas and run a red light, throwing her middle finger out the window with trademark defiance. Stupid. What a stupid thing to do. Now a whole fucking SWAT team was after her.

*Well, if it's me, it's not you, lamb.*

*I know I hurt you, but you're still alive.*

*Try and stay that way.*

Sadie reached the Sonoma city limit and headed north, winding her way through the vineyard valleys and tiny towns like a damn tourist. The wide river was on her left, and rays of the rising sun shot out from behind the clouds to cast a red-pink glow off the water. This day would bring more heat for the dying vines.

More decay.

More loss.

Sadie squared her shoulders and gritted her teeth. The highway wasn't far. She could make it, she thought. She could lose them. From there, she didn't know where she'd go—to the sea, to the mountains—but maybe she didn't need to know. Maybe for once she could take things as they came to her. React. Not act.

Not seek to destroy.

Another glance in the rearview mirror. The police cars were still there, as close as ever, a whole goddamn cop parade, like it was a national holiday or something.

"Fuck you," Sadie snarled. Didn't they have anything better to do? The stoplight ahead of her turned yellow, but as always, Sadie and caution were like oil and water.

She went for it, blowing through the intersection amid a blare of horns and screeching tires. Only the vehicles behind her didn't stop. They just followed with terrible persistence.

They kept following.

Sadie slammed her hand on the dash in frustration. The highway was visible in the distance now. She sped toward it, but the closer she got, the better she was able to see the streaks of squad cars, dozens of them, that were peeling down it, from both directions. All heading straight for the road she was on.

There was no escape.

None.

Sadie's chest ached and heaved. She looked around, at the gun, the blood, and she understood the inevitability of the situation. The direness. Some actions you couldn't take back. Some events you were powerless to stop. There was only one way this would end, and in the pounding of her pulse and the sweat dripping down her brow, Sadie was beginning to feel things she'd never felt before.

Like fear.

Like despair.

But also hope, a tiny, sparkling glimmer of it.

*Is this love?*

*Is that what this is?*

Her eyes stung, but Sadie kept going. Another mile. Then another. She pushed it and pushed it and pushed it, until there was nothing left to push. The oncoming police vehicles were in front of her now, the distance between them closing fast. With a ragged gasp, she yanked the steering wheel as hard as she could, twisting it to the right as she hit the brakes. The car wobbled, then fishtailed, revolving nose around nose, before skidding onto the shoulder and coming to a shuddering stop. She grabbed for the gun beside her.

Dust from the roadside swirled up and over the Jetta, clouding the windows with something hazy and thick, reminding Sadie of the way morning mist might swirl over a moat that led to the most impenetrable of castles—a fortress built of stone and faith that was meant to endure for the ages.

As the haze settled, cops scrambled from their cars, both in front and behind her. They had their sirens on, their lights still going. They shouted at her. They crouched down low. They drew their weapons.

This was it, then. Her time was up. Over. Done.

There would be no more chasing peace. No more boredom.

The world would move on without her.

A small sob escaped Sadie's lips. She wasn't scared, not really—she'd never been one to surrender. But she hadn't known how much the end would hurt.

It was all the more sweet for the pain, though. That was the last thing Sadie thought before shoving the car door open and launching herself into the dust and the heat, with the rosewood butt of her father's gleaming rifle hooked over one shoulder. What she had, and what Miles would because of her, why that was the point of it all.

Wasn't that a *brilliant* thing?

She'd had her shine.

And now, somewhere, somehow, for a heart she'd never know, to light a sky she'd never see, someone else was preparing for theirs.